FALL FROM GRACE

A DCI HARRY MCNEIL NOVEL

JOHN CARSON

D1534071

DCI SEAN BRACKEN SERIES

DCI HARRY MCNEIL SERIES

DI FRANK MILLER SERIES

Crash Point

Silent Marker

Rain Town

Watch Me Bleed

Broken Wheels

Sudden Death

Under the Knife

Trial and Error

Warning Sign

Cut Throat

Blood from a Stone

Time of Death

Frank Miller Crime Series – Books 1-3 – Box set

Frank Miller Crime Series - Books 4-6 - Box set

MAX DOYLE SERIES

SCOTT MARSHALL SERIES

Old Habits

FALL FROM GRACE

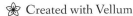 Created with Vellum

To Charlie Wilson, for all her hard work.

ONE

Sergeant Bobby McGuire was going to die.

First, though, his lungs would implode and his legs would go on fire. Or was it the other way around?

His legs pushed the pedals on the bike, and he tried to look at the top of the hill, imagining there was a nice cold drink waiting for him up there if he was lucky. Or a coffin if he wasn't.

There was a defibrillator back at the station, but that wouldn't do him much good when he was going to die halfway up Cardiac Brae.

He wished the bike had one of those wee baskets on the front. That would save him having to pull over to the side of the road to puke in the nettles.

They had two patrol cars and both constables were out in them. Both were busy and both were going to get a boot in the bollocks.

The call had come in twenty minutes ago, necessitating the use of what was affectionately known in the station as *that bastard bike*. The piece of lost property that nobody in his right mind would claim.

Of course, McGuire had never ridden the bike before. It was a ratty thing that was well and truly past its prime. He'd seen better looking shopping trolleys after they'd been pulled out of the river. It had sat in lost property since it had presumably fallen off the Ark and had washed up on the shore.

The thing with the bike was, it didn't free-wheel. McGuire wasn't technically minded, but every bike he'd ever ridden had wheels that still went round after you stopped pedalling.

He hadn't noticed this fault with the bike until he'd made it halfway to his destination. To say the bike was going to be scrapped after this was an understatement. A swift kicking round the back of the station with a hammer was more likely. To render it useless to any future officer. Or maybe he should make that pair of useless bastards ride it for a few weeks. Teach them a bloody lesson.

He heard the sound of a car coming behind him and risked a look over his right shoulder. Christ, it was Tam the Bam, heading straight for him in his old dark-green Morris Minor.

At the last minute, Tam swerved out of McGuire's way and pulled into the side of the road.

McGuire had jumped off the bike at this point, which wasn't as hard as it sounded as he was only cycling at walking speed. A toddler's walking speed.

Tam got out of his car, laughing. 'You might want to watch yourself there, Bobby. I nearly had Bessy over the top of you.'

McGuire couldn't quite catch enough breath to call Tam an arsehole, so he stood and tried to catch his breath and get his shaking legs under control.

Tam was obviously one of those bastards who gave their car a name. Who in the name of God was *Bessy*?

'You nearly had me over that fucking wall, Tam,' McGuire said when his lungs would allow him to speak.

'I saw you. I was distracted by seeing you struggle.'

'Magic. At least I know you were around to call for an ambulance after you skelped me.'

Tam laughed. He was a bit older than McGuire's forty-five, but as for pinning down an exact age, nobody really knew for sure.

'Where are you going on that old thing?' Tam asked, the idiot grin fixed firmly on his face. Something that McGuire was five seconds away from wiping off.

'Old Kirk graveyard.'

'Flowers for your old gran?'

McGuire looked at the other man, and the sweat was running into his eyes. 'You think I'd be cycling up this fucking hill to put flowers on my grannie's grave? Besides, she was cremated, Tam. And do you see flowers in my hand?'

The sun was out and it was only the slight breeze McGuire felt that was keeping the cardiac episode at bay. The hills in the distance looked inviting to hikers he was sure, but looking at them from his own perspective made him want to puke.

'Right, let me in the passenger seat. I'm knackered.' McGuire picked up the bike and threw it over the wall.

'Perfectly good bike that,' Tam said.

'Feel free to come back and get it then.' McGuire got into what was more like a time machine than a car. It had a strap to pull the door closed. Tam climbed in behind the wheel.

'You're not going to be too long, are ye, Bobby? I mean, I'm fine with you having a wee rest, but I'm late for an appointment.'

'You're going to drive me to the graveyard, wait for me, then drive me back to the station.'

That wiped the smile off Tam's face without any need for violence. 'Oh, well, as much as I'd like to, Sergeant...'

'Listen here, Tam, because I'm only going to say this once: I can either retrieve that bike and cycle the rest of the way and back again, or you can give me a lift. If I have to cycle, this is what's going to happen: next time you're in the Stag's Head, getting pished out of your skull, and you come out and get behind the wheel of this fucking death trap, I will pull you over and ream you a new arsehole. I will make sure you not only lose your licence but you never fucking drive again. There will be no eyes turned, blind or otherwise. There will be no, *Watch what you're doing on the way home, Tam.* I will, for all intents and purposes, have rammed a night stick up your arse. All the bonhomie will be gone. I will pull you over every time I feel like it, and if there's even the tiniest whiff of a Polo mint on your breath, I will assume you've been at the bottle. Like now.'

'I've not been eating Polo mints,' Tam protested.

'You fucking should have been! Your breath smells like the tail end of a distillery tour. Almost knocking a police officer off a bike while he was working might not be a hanging offence, but by the time I'm finished, you'll wish you had built your own gallows.'

'I never knocked you off your bike.'

'It's over that wall there. Who are they going to believe? A respected sergeant, or some alkie who witnesses will say was in the pub knocking it back until he got behind the wheel of his car and took off?'

Tam made the mistake of blowing his breath out

into the car. 'I have to say, I'm offended, Bobby. All you
had to do was ask.'

McGuire could feel his heart racing and prayed it
wasn't going to give out right now. He had no doubt the
other man would drag his lifeless corpse out of the tin
Lizzy and leave it by the side of the road after fetching
that bastard bike from behind the wall.

'Let's go, Tam. I'm not saying your car is slow, but I
want to get to the graveyard before I have to go
Christmas shopping and the summer solstice hasn't
even hit yet.'

McGuire looked at the keychain hanging from the
ignition key in the middle of the dash, below the
speedometer. Tam put the car in gear and took the
handbrake off, and the old car lurched up the hill.
Very little traffic came up here, except maybe farm
vehicles, and McGuire knew his body would only
have been discovered by chance if he'd popped his
clogs here.

'I suppose it's pointless asking if this thing has air
conditioning?' McGuire asked, feeling rivers of sweat
running down parts of his body that he couldn't even
see in a mirror.

Tam laughed. 'See that little triangular window?
That's called a side light. Push the button, swing the
lever and it opens. That's your air conditioning. If you
want it on full blast, wind the big window down.'

McGuire tried the side light first, having no idea why a little window would be called a light.

'That's genius,' he said. 'Air conditioning *and* a midge catcher all in one. May as well go out with a bang.' He rolled the window down. The air was cool and hit his face with enough slapping power to ward off any impending recuperation in an intensive care ward.

To McGuire's uninitiated ears, the small engine could have beaten a Chieftain tank for noisiest bastard machine on the planet, but the rushing of blood in his ears had subsided as they crested the top of the hill and he was glad to see there was no coffin waiting, imaginary or otherwise.

Tam turned left and suddenly the car was going faster, like they were on a roller coaster.

'You don't need fancy technology to enjoy a car,' he said as the thin tyres scrabbled for purchase going round a right-hand bend at the foot of the hill.

'Fancy technology?' McGuire said. 'Like working brakes?'

To give the wee car its due, the momentum carried it up the next hill and round the left-hand bend, and now they were on the straightaway, going under a canopy of trees that offered relief from the Highland sun. It wasn't Majorca temperatures, but Scotland could still make you sweat if you wore all the clothing you had been told to pack for all the seasons you would experience in one day.

McGuire was expecting Tam to start braking, and when he looked over, he saw the older man's foot *was* on the brake.

'The entrance up on the left,' he said, hoping the man was just tickling the brake pedal in expectation of giving it his full weight.

'I know,' Tam replied, his tongue sticking out of the corner of his mouth, as if full concentration was needed at this point before they took down part of the wall.

'Jesus,' McGuire said, closing his eyes just before the impact he felt was coming. But the small car was through the opening and bumping over the ruts that used to be a track before McGuire had had the chance to ask Tam to tell his wife he loved her. But then, Tam would have been a goner too.

The Minor – McGuire refused to call the damn thing *Bessy* – rolled to a stop, with Tam putting as much weight on the brake pedal as he could muster. The policeman wondered just how in God's name Tam got home in one piece when he was drunk driving. The phrase *'wing and a prayer'* sprang to mind.

'Which way?' Tam asked, looking over at the old church sitting silently on their right. Boarded up and abandoned for years now, it sat forlornly, looking down on the occupants of the graveyard. Their final resting place now resembled an overgrown field.

'Somewhere over there,' McGuire answered, 'but you stay in the car. This is something I have to check out myself.'

'Suit yourself, Sergeant McGuire, sir,' Tam said. McGuire looked at him for a moment to see if he was taking the piss, but then he realised the older man was doing his pitch for, *Please don't have me rely on those taxi-driving bastards.*

The trees were large, overgrown and had been left to their own devices. A wind that McGuire hadn't felt just a few minutes ago now animated the grass and branches. He walked round the back of the car – mostly to take away any temptation Tam had of running him over – and walked along a track that was overgrown but still had some of the red stone chips that had been laid years ago in a futile attempt to create a proper road.

He approached the church. The door was facing him and he was surprised to see there was no graffiti on it. The wee bastards nowadays would graffiti their own fucking ho, but the old building had been spared. Maybe they were too scared to come here after dark.

McGuire was apprehensive coming here *before*

dark, but at least he had a baton on his waist that would give him half a chance.

He turned left, heading south. It wasn't a large cemetery but was large enough to accommodate locals from all around.

Another canopy of trees blocked the sun, and McGuire wished he had told Tam to come with him. He wasn't scared, but what if there was somebody here? Like, a gang of bikers?

'Shut up, McGuire,' he scolded himself. Gang of bikers indeed.

The pathway turned right and left, but he knew he had to take the right path, because that was where the people had said their daughter had run to. There was an archway in the stone wall. A very long time ago, the cemetery had reached maximum capacity, and membership had to be denied to those who had died. Whoever oversaw these matters decided that an extension had to be built, and this was where McGuire had to go and look.

More old trees, more overgrown grass. He had asked, what was she doing in here? *Nightmare* was the answer. Christ, more ghouls, all of them hoping to catch sight of the elusive figure who didn't even exist.

Clouds had come scudding over, obscuring the light. Dark clouds, bringing the threat of rain. He hoped Tam was still waiting when he got back, but he suspected the man would be. Or else his life would be a living hell.

McGuire took out a piece of paper from his pocket. *Through the arch, turn right, first pathway on the left.*

It was like being on one of those stupid game shows where you had to find something for the chance to win an old kettle and a year's subscription to a comic. Some such shite.

This path could hardly be called beaten anymore. Long grass tugged at his trousers, as if trying to trip him. He took his baton out, keeping a tight grip on it.

'What are you going to do with that?' a voice said from behind him.

McGuire spun, bringing the baton up, and was about to bring it down on the head of the man standing behind him.

'Fucking hell, Tam. I thought I said to stay in the car?' His voice had more relief than anger in it.

'I was bored.'

'Scared shitless, more like.'

'Away with yourself. I thought I would back you up if somebody was creeping about here.'

'Just don't touch anything.'

Tam made a face and looked around him. 'What's there to touch? Manky old gravestones?'

'I have to go down here,' McGuire said, nodding to the path on his left. There was where the old mausoleums were. *Millionaire's row.* The last resting places of business owners from around these parts.

'I'll follow you. I'll give a wee cough, so you don't shit yourself again.'

Apparently, all thoughts of losing his licence were now gone, McGuire thought, seeing the big grin on Tam's face.

The sergeant couldn't think of a suitable retort, so he kept his eyes on the mausoleums. Should they make a noise, alert anybody who was here? What if some gypsies had set up camp here? Some Devil worshippers?

'There!' Tam blurted out in a high voice, any hope of a covert approach now out the window.

He could see a shoe sticking out from the side of the first mausoleum. It was white, lying on its side. A trainer.

McGuire edged forward. 'Watch our backs, Tam.'

'Gotcha.'

The sergeant edged forward to the old marble death house and brought the baton up over his shoulder. The *hit them on the shoulder* he'd been trained to do was the last thing on his mind. He'd swing the bastard thing about like a maniac if somebody came at him with a knife.

He didn't approach the wayward shoe but stepped further along the path and looked round.

It was only a shoe.

He looked past it to where the perimeter wall should be but only saw overgrown grass and bushes. He knew the wall was there, but this new part of the cemetery was in just as bad a shape as the old part. He couldn't even see the spire of the church for the canopy of trees overhead.

He moved forward along the path and gave a quick look round to make sure Tam hadn't scarpered, feeling relief when he saw he hadn't.

'Who do you think the shoe belongs to?' Tam asked. 'It looks pretty new.'

'The person I'm looking for.'

McGuire stepped past the next mausoleum and there she was. Even though he was half expecting to find somebody, it would have been a relief to have reported back that there was nobody here.

But there was.

She was lying face down. Her long brown hair flowed out from her head and partially laid on the back of her red jacket. He saw where the other white trainer was: still attached to her foot.

He wondered why she had chosen to wear red in here. So she could easily be seen by rescuers? But if there had been somebody watching here, this wasn't exactly camo.

He walked up to her and turned round.

'Tam, stay there. If this is a crime scene, we can't have it contaminated.' He saw that Tam hadn't moved but was looking at the girl.

'Is she dead?'

Thoughts of *How the fuck should I know?* to *I forgot my crystal ball* and everything in between ran through McGuire's head, but he said nothing more derogatory than, 'Give me a minute.'

The sergeant slipped his baton back and reached down to gently roll the girl over. He jumped back a bit as he looked down at the slash mark across her neck.

Tam turned and heaved into the long grass.

McGuire looked at her, but it wasn't the wound in her neck that he was staring at.

It was the words carved into her chest:

I am Nightmare.

TWO

Ian Flucker had burnt his toast, which seemed appropriate considering who was going to be his first patient this morning. He didn't like calling them patients, more like clients. Customers was a definite no-no.

This first client had a penchant for playing with fire.

He took the toast and scraped the blackness from the bread into the sink and quickly ran the water before his wife came down. The last thing he needed was her nagging at him again.

'Relax, Ian, you're a bloody psychologist. It's your job to talk people off the ledge and keep them calm,' he told himself.

He took the charred offering back to the table and buttered it. Real butter, mind, none of that fake crap. If you were going to harden your arteries, it was best to at least enjoy yourself. The gym eluded him, and jogging held as much appeal as an overripe banana. Some of which were still sitting in the fruit bowl, like he and his wife were having a mental showdown over them. Who was going to throw them away first?

The radio played in the background.

'Did you burn the toast again?' Linda said as she came into the kitchen.

He thought about lying to her, but the last time he'd done that, he'd compounded it with another lie and it had got away from him.

'What gave it away? The smell or the black edges?'

'No need to be snarky, love,' she said.

Apologise or not apologise? That was the question. 'Sorry, honey, I'm just feeling stressed.' Fuck it. He didn't need her being in a strop when he got home. It was Friday, the lead-up to the weekend, and the last thing he wanted to do was get her in a mood before they went out for their Indian tonight. Ruby Murray, couple of bottles of wine and then upstairs for a bit of how's your father. If he was feeling adventurous, he'd splash on some Old Spice and change his underwear.

'You haven't forgotten about tomorrow night?' Linda said.

Flucker almost had to ram the butter knife into his hand to stop the runaway reply firing out of his mouth, but he dug deep. *Go with the flow.*

'No, I haven't forgotten. I'm looking forward to it, actually.'

'Are you? I thought you said the last time that Dave was a dick.'

'He is. But I feel sorry for Maureen, so if we go along, she has company other than her boring bastard of a husband to look at.'

'Try not to make any sarcastic comments like the last time.' Linda poured herself a coffee and sat at the table opposite her husband.

'I was merely making an observation. If it sounded like sarcasm, then that's not my fault. I deal with people like him all the time. If he doesn't like somebody, he'll stay quiet and let the other person think of a topic of conversation.'

'It must be an illness. He never used to be like that.'

'It is a sort of illness; it's called Ignorus Wankerous.'

'Is it? I've never heard of that.'

Flucker closed his eyes for a moment. He was expecting to be shot down in flames for that one, but maybe she'd be driving to work along the Great Western Road and it would hit her.

Dave Sangster. Loosely rhymed with wanker. Flucker understood with his training he should know better, and to let Dave's indifference slide off him, but the man was so arrogant. Dave and Maureen lived in a semi-detached and he drove an old Golf while she hoofed it or took the bus. Yet they looked down on Flucker and Linda. Especially the wife. Because her family had money, she thought she was big time, but she was a civil servant like his Linda.

'Try and remember to get a couple of bottles of wine on your way home, love. And the beer.' Linda sipped her coffee, no doubt gasping for a cigarette but she daren't, not after Flucker had gone out of his way to help her kick the habit. She would be about ready to chew a leg off the kitchen table by the time he left, but fuck her. He could put her out of her misery by suggesting she go into the back garden for a quick puff, but why should he? She had poo-pooed his suggestion they go to a swingers' party.

The idea of her wanting a cigarette just made his agony increase. His first client. No, patient. He'd be damned if he'd gone to medical school for all those years just to mollycoddle those fuckers. They were daft, plain and simple, and they needed to come and see him so he could mentally hold their hand and talk all cooey-cooey to them.

Not all of them were daft, mind. But the first one was.

'Do I have any whisky left?' he asked Linda.

'How should I know? I don't drink the stuff.'

'Since you're driving tomorrow night, I'm going to need a few swifties before we go.'

'Just don't walk in half-jaked like the last time. No wonder Dave didn't speak much. I think he'd passed out from the fumes coming out of your mouth.'

'Yeah, that's why he didn't talk.' *Nothing to do with the fact he's an ignorant bastard.*

Flucker got up from the table and ran the plate under the tap, trying to get the black crumbs off it, but the wee bastards didn't want to play, so he gave up and put the plate in the dishwasher.

Then he left the house.

The drive to Helen Street station wasn't that long, but it felt like an age. Ever since he had taken on this part of his job, he'd wished he had poked his eye out with a stick instead.

Counselling police officers wasn't exactly at the top of his tree. He felt guilty for thinking this way, and most of them benefitted from his experience, but there were some who had the attitude that they shouldn't be here, it was a waste of time and they were harder than anybody.

Some of those same men and women then sat and cried in his office.

His first client was an anomaly. Shot twice, years ago. That would certainly have put *him* off, but this man had gone about like nothing had happened afterwards. Maybe his time in the army had served him well. Maybe he was just mental.

He let on to the man at the gatehouse and parked in a reserved spot before heading upstairs.

He looked at his watch as he walked along the corridor to his office. Ten minutes to spare before the next hour of pure hell.

He stepped into the waiting room by his office and stopped short.

Fuck. He was early.

His first client sat on one of the chairs. There was always a ten-minute period between each session, so that the previous officer could have time to leave without being seen by his or her colleagues, but he was the first one so there was no need for stealth.

'Mornin', Doc,' Detective Superintendent Calvin Stewart said.

'Good morning, Calvin.' Flucker insisted on first name terms. It was too much of a rigmarole saying their rank first, so that was his rule. It meant they were all on a level playing field.

'Give me a min–' he started to say, but Stewart was right in behind him before he'd even got the door fully open. The big mongo had started early.

'I'll get that fucking coffee machine belting away,' he said, and Flucker stopped and held up a hand.

'Remember what we talked about last time, Calvin?'

'Oh fuck, aye; I've to stop swearing. Oh shite, there I go again. But I have been working on it.'

'Good. Try harder.' Flucker took his jacket off while Stewart plugged the machine in and pressed the *on* button.

When it had heated up, Stewart took one of the little K cups and lifted the lid on the machine and inserted it. After a couple of minutes, the coffee was ready.

'You up for one, boss?' Stewart said.

'Aye, go on then. Strong, and not that caramel junk you put in last time.'

'In my own defence, it was you who put that pish in the wee cup holder.'

'Let's not make that mistake again then, shall we?'

'Whatever you say.' Stewart added creamer while he put Flucker's K cup in. 'I've got a mouth like a camel's arse. One too many last night. It doesn't matter, though, since you're recommending I get the bullet anyway.'

Flucker sat on his chair, opposite the patient's leather chair; it was all set up for doctor and client to sit in a relaxing atmosphere. 'You've already had two bullets, Calvin. I don't think you need a third.'

'Try telling that to the high heid yins. There are a

lot of bottom feeders who would throw a party if I left, and it wouldn't be for me.'

Stewart added creamer to his own coffee and sat down opposite Flucker, handing him the cup.

'You still have the feeling that everybody is out to get you, Calvin?'

'What? No. Don't say it like I'm some daft wee laddie.'

'You said that the forensics chief was out to get you.'

'Fudboy? He's a wee rat.'

'Finbar. Yes, some people might think that way,' Flucker said.

'He made a complaint against me. Everybody slags each other off, but he takes it personally.'

'You said to him, quote, *I'll ram a fucking hedgehog up your arse.* Unquote.'

Stewart took his lighter out of his pocket and held his thumb over the wheel. 'He's an annoying little cu–'

Flucker held up a finger, taking the interruption time to have a sip of coffee.

'Aye, I know. Swearing. Anyway, he's an annoying little fanny and he gets me in the crapper. Bloody nerve.'

Flucker put his cup down on a side table. 'You've been doing well recently, but I think you need a little break.'

'I've been told I'll be getting a permanent holiday soon. I don't fit in with the new way of policing.'

'As I said, you need a break. That's why I'm recommending in my weekly report that you have a change of scenery.'

'They won't approve that. We're too busy here.'

'Trust me, when I write this report, they'll be seeing you off on the train.'

THREE

Two months earlier

'I'm going to die, Harry,' Alex said, gripping his hand like she was practising for the arm-wrestling world championship.

'You're going to be fine, honey. I'm here.'

Detective Chief Inspector Harry McNeil was looking down at his wife and thinking how he couldn't have loved her more at that moment. It had been four hours from the time her water broke until this moment. They had been expecting closer to *twenty*-four hours, but their little girl was coming into this world at high speed.

'I need an epidural,' Alex said to the midwife.

'Honey, by the time that kicked in, the wee one will

be here.'

'Give me some gas. Please.'

The midwife gave her the mask to hold, then she told her to give one more big push.

Harry looked down and suddenly his daughter was being born, and he had the strangest feeling come over him. Now he understood why some men fainted at witnessing their child coming into the world. The room swam for a moment, and he thought the floor was going to come at him and slap his jaw.

At the same time it hit him, it passed. The baby looked blue to his eyes, like something was wrong, but then the midwife was by his side, holding a pair of scissors like there was some ribbon to be cut. But it was the umbilical cord she wanted him to cut.

'It won't hurt her?' he asked.

A look passed between the midwife and Alex, but he ignored them.

'No, she won't feel it,' the midwife assured him. She held the cord in two places, guiding him to a spot where he should cut it, just in case his spatial awareness wasn't up to scratch.

He gingerly cut the cord like he was cutting the red wire on a bomb. Snip, close your eyes and hope for the best. Bomb-defusing 101.

He stood and smiled and looked away for a second. This was a close second to his hatred of being in the mortuary when a dead person needed to be examined internally with the aid of rib spreaders.

The baby was wrapped in a towel and taken out of the room for a moment to be weighed.

'She's beautiful, our little Amy,' Harry said.

'I was thinking about that, sweetheart. Do you think we could name her Grace? After my granny?'

Harry didn't know what to say for a moment. He'd thought of his unborn daughter as Amy all this time, and the sudden, last-minute change took him by surprise.

The midwife came back in with their daughter. 'Seven pounds, five ounces. Do you have a name for her?' *Or are you a couple of modern fuckwits who don't acknowledge your child has a sex and thinks they should choose their own name when they go to high school?*

The look was there if the question wasn't.

'Grace,' Harry said, smiling at his wife, glad she hadn't come out with *Bubble bath fruit basket* like they were Hollywood celebrities.

'Grace Amy McNeil,' Alex said.

Harry smiled at her. As far as he knew, there wasn't an Amy in his family, but it had been a name they had both agreed on.

Alex grabbed hold of his hand and squeezed.

FOUR

Present day

Alex had asked him once, *What would you do if this was our last day together?*

Harry McNeil didn't have an immediate answer for his wife. He knew he would want to spend every minute with her, but had she meant, there's a meteor going to crash into earth, or, are we walking away from our marriage?

With his baby daughter lying sleeping in his arms as he sat on the couch, he didn't want to think about it. It reminded him of the song by Depeche Mode, 'Enjoy the Silence'. Everything he needed was right here. His wife and his daughter.

Alex turned to him and took her phone out, opening the camera, and took another photo.

'You two look so comfortable,' she said to him.

'I'm nodding off,' Harry replied, and it was true. Something about the little bundle of warmth was making him want to take a nap.

'Well, you can't. You have to go on your wee holiday up north.'

'Holiday, or murder investigation? It's a toss-up what's more fun.'

'Either way, you get to go. I have one more week then I'm back at work.' She looked sad.

'You like being home with Grace, though, don't you?'

'I do. I also liked being a detective. I've had more time off than I should have.'

'Nonsense. Your body was telling you to take it easy. You just needed time off to rest and make sure our wee girl came into the world safely.' He looked at her. 'Why don't you give it some more consideration? What we talked about.'

Alex blew her breath out, puffing her cheeks. 'I honestly don't know if I could be a full-time mum, Harry. I don't want to make a rash decision.'

'We have a small mortgage. I can take care of that. And everything else.'

'Let me think about it some more. I've been looking at nannies. Some of them come highly qualified.'

'I'm sure they do. But all I'm saying is, you have the option to stay at home if you want to. If you want to go back to work, then that's fine too.'

He smiled at his daughter, still sleeping in his arms.

'I honestly thought you were going to faint when I saw your face,' Alex said.

'For the hundredth time, it was warm in there, that's all. I wish that I had been able to attend Chance's birth. That would have been practice for Grace's, but I was working at the time and my ex had given birth by the time I got there.'

'She didn't beat four hours, though, did she?' Alex said with a smile, quite proud of herself.

'No, and I don't believe she told the midwife to go fuck herself either.'

'I was out of it. I needed more gas and she was slow. It wasn't anything personal.'

'Four hours from start to finish. I've been at a water park in Spain that lasted longer.' He smiled at her. 'You see what I did there? Referenced the water park, because of the slipping down a wet –'

'I get the idea,' Alex said, cutting him off. 'But you'd better get your stuff ready for tomorrow.'

'It's not going to be the same without you.'

'I know. You, Jimmy and Robbie up in the High-lands, all work and no play.'

'Well, maybe a light refreshment in the bar after work. It's hot up there too in the summer.'

'No, it's not. It'll be pishing down every day, with the odd peek of the sun.'

'That's true. We'll only be in the bar to regroup.'

'Well, our daughter and I will be here, regrouping every day, with baby milk and coffee being the strongest drinks.'

'I don't think Grace is old enough for coffee, honey.'

Alex shook her head. 'Your dad won't change, Grace. You're stuck with him, I'm afraid.'

The baby moved as if she had heard, then went back to sleep. For thirty seconds, until the doorbell rang.

Harry's brother, Derek, came in with their sister, Mel.

'There she is,' Mel said, smiling down at Grace, who was awake now. She took the baby from Harry. 'Hello, my wee darling,' she said.

'I was about to make coffee,' Alex said. 'Would you both like a cup?'

'Thanks, Alex. I'll come through to the kitchen with you.'

The women left the living room and Derek sat at

the little table for two at the window.

'You settling down to fatherhood again then, brother?'

'It was easier when I was younger, but it's not too bad. She's worth it.'

'Aye, she is that.'

'Any sign of you and Briony having one?'

'What? Away, man. We're fine just as we are. She apologises for not being here today, but she's doing a double shift.' Derek's girlfriend was a nurse.

'No problem. We'll go for a Chinese one night. Alex's sister, Jessica, said she would babysit anytime for us.'

'Smashing. How about tomorrow night?' Derek asked.

'Sorry, pal. No can do. I'm off to Inverness in the morning.'

'Inverness? On your own?'

'Aye. Inverness MIT are stretched to the limit, so they've asked us to go up and give them a hand. Extra manpower.'

'What's the case?'

Harry looked at his brother for a moment, wondering how best to tell him.

'Remember the Nightmare Man? The scary man that Mum used to scare us with? *Get to bed or the Nightmare Man will come and get you?*'

'How could I forget?'

'Then years later, three girls were found dead with *I am Nightmare* carved into their chest?'

'Aye, I remember that.'

'Seems like he's back. A young woman was found dead in a cemetery in a small town west of Inverness.'

'The same place?'

'It is. The old graveyard is overgrown and not used anymore. She was found there. They want us up there tomorrow.'

'We didn't live there at the time, though, did we?'

Harry looked solemn. 'Yes, we did. Then six months later, Dad transferred to Fife Constabulary and we moved to Glenrothes. You remember now? I was twelve, you were ten and Mel was eight.'

'Oh aye, I remember now. I used to shite myself after Mum said the Nightmare Man would come and get me in my sleep. Especially after he killed those lassies.'

'That was almost thirty years ago.'

'It can't be the same bloke, though, surely?' Derek said.

'Who knows? What if the killer back then was twenty-five? He'd be in his fifties now, still physically able to kill a young woman.'

'Jesus. That doesn't bear thinking about.'

'Or it might just be somebody else who heard the

story. The legend and the killings. Whatever it is, we need to get to the bottom of it.'

'Unlike Dad. His lot couldn't find a bag of sweeties in a paedo's car outside a primary school.'

'Don't talk like that, for fuck's sake. Dad wasn't the only detective.'

'You know what I mean. Yes, there are serious crimes up there, but they're few and far between, aren't they?'

Harry shook his head. 'When's the last time you were up in Inverness? They have drugs up there, believe it or not. Prostitutes, robbers. Don't make it sound like Victorian times.'

'At least they knew how to take care of them back in the day.'

'We're not having this conversation again, are we, Derek?' Harry said.

His brother spread his hands. 'I'm just saying. There has to be a deterrent or else those wee bastards will take over the place.'

'Meantime, we have to make do with what we have.'

'I'm just saying, apart from that nut job going about up there when we were laddies, I remember it being a nice place to live.'

'Fife was okay too,' Harry said. 'I have good memories of living in Dunfermline. Like going to Burntisland shows on the Links. And the beach.'

Derek chuckled. 'Aye, we had some good times down there. Especially when we were teenagers. We used to chorey Dad's beer and meet up with those lassies.'

'Good times indeed.'

'Maybe I should come up to Inverness with you. I have my own business now, so I can take some time off.'

'It's not a hooley we're going on, Derek. A lassie's been murdered.'

'Aye, I know that, but you and the others have to get some time off, don't you? A wee swally in the bar at night, that sort of thing. I wouldn't mind just having a wee look around while you're doing your investigation stuff.'

'Christ, I can't sanction that.'

Derek smiled at him. 'I know you can't. But there's no law against me going to Inverness to visit my old Auntie Ella.'

'We were planning on taking Grace to see her over the summer. I'm sure she'll be just as pleased to see the other bairn,' Harry said.

'What other bairn? Chance?'

'No, ya clown; you.'

'Oh aye. I knew that. So, what do you say?'

Harry shrugged. 'As I said, I can't stop you going

up to Inverness. It's a free country. What would Briony say?'

'Nothing. I'll tell her I want to take a trip with my big brother. If nobody happens to mention that he's investigating a murder –'

Harry put up a hand. 'Let me stop you there. Briony isn't stupid. In fact, she's a lot more intelligent than you. No offence.'

'I can't argue with that.'

'She'll know I wouldn't be swanning off to Inverness and leaving my wife and two-month-old baby behind.'

Derek stared off into space for a moment. Then he snapped his fingers. 'I'll just tell her you're going there on business and I asked to tag along so we could go and see Auntie Ella.'

'You do what you want, brother. All I know is, I'm leaving at eight tomorrow morning.'

Derek looked sheepishly at him. 'I don't suppose you could swing by Dalgety Bay?'

Harry shook his head. 'One minute late and I'm leaving without you.'

Derek beamed a smile. 'I'll even set my alarm.'

The women came back in with baby Grace. 'What are you two conspiring about?' Alex asked.

Derek looked at her. 'Do you want to tell her or will I?'

FIVE

'Have you been a bawbag again?' DCI Jimmy Dunbar asked as he and DS Robbie Evans stood outside DSup Calvin Stewart's office in the Helen Street station.

'How come I'm the bawbag?'

'We're supposed to be on the road by now, but then I get a call from DSup McKenzie saying she wants a word with us. And why didn't Stewart want a word?'

'Maybe he's popped his clogs,' Evans replied.

'Aye, you'd like that, wouldn't you, ya wee bastard,' a voice boomed from behind them.

'Christ, you might have told me he was coming,' Evans complained in a low voice.

'I would have if I'd known.'

Stewart caught up with them. 'Sorry to disappoint you, son, but I have no intention of *popping my fucking clogs* as you so eloquently put it.'

Dunbar looked at him. 'We're here to see DSup McKenzie, sir. I didn't realise you would be here too.'

'What, Lynn didn't tell you I was coming? That was remiss of her. I'll need to give her a wee talking-to about this. Tell her you're kicking up a stink out here. Calling her all sorts of names.'

Several images ran through Dunbar's mind, all of them quiet locations where he could bury Stewart and nobody would ever find him.

'Relax, Jimmy, I'm pulling your leg. She said we should go in when I got here.' Stewart looked at his watch. 'I've surprised myself by getting here on time. My therapist said to try harder with my timekeeping. He's going to be proud. Less swearing, better timekeeping. I wonder what other surprises I can pull out of my hat.'

'Buying a round might go a long way to convincing us you're a changed man,' Dunbar said.

Stewart laughed. 'Easy there, son. Baby steps. I don't want it to be too much of a culture shock for you.' He stepped forward and knocked on the door, and they all heard DSup McKenzie tell them to enter.

Dunbar led the charge, with Evans closing the door behind the posse.

'DSup Stewart. Thank you for coming in on your day off,' Lynn McKenzie said, smiling at him from behind the desk, but it was the sort of smile that might have been reserved for a nephew whose magic trick was to set the curtains on fire.

'Any time, DSup McKenzie.'

Dunbar wondered if this calling each other by their rank had been rehearsed beforehand, or whether they were each making sure they knew they were both of equal stature.

'Please, have a seat,' she said, indicating the two chairs on the other side of the trench. No Man's Land, where one of them was going to have to be the third one to smoke the cigarette.

Evans didn't bother to try to sit down. The two officers sat down and faced the woman, who looked like she could have done well at any profession she chose. She was wearing a red shirt and dark trousers, very much a professional while keeping it casual.

'Did you tell Dunbar and Evans?' she asked Stewart.

'Not yet. I thought it best to wait.'

'Tell us what?' Dunbar said. Please let it be, *The man in the next bed wants to buy his slippers.*

'I briefed you and DS Evans last night about the job in Inverness. However – and I have to warn you that this is not to go further than this office – DSup Stewart is going with you.'

Dunbar did a good impression of a grown man trying not to cry.

'I will be responsible for the day-to-day running of this office while you're all gone. It's unusual for a high-ranking officer to be seconded, but that's what's happening today. No explanation is needed or offered. The three of you will leave right away. The pool car is waiting,' McKenzie said, procuring a set of car keys from her desk drawer and laying them on her desk. 'Don't crash it, race it, wreck it or leave it smelling like a Bangkok whorehouse. And no, I've never been in a Bangkok whorehouse, but use your imagination.'

Dunbar looked at her like he was waiting for her to burst out laughing and tell them she was only having a laugh, but when this didn't happen and he blinked first, he took the keys and passed them to Evans, who stepped forward to take them.

'In general,' McKenzie said, 'don't bring it back in a cardboard box.' She looked at Stewart. 'Daily report around five-ish. If I don't get the call, I will assume you're up to your ears fighting crime. I had better not even remotely see a glass of alcohol when we do the video chat.'

'You know me better than that, Lynn,' Stewart said, deciding that being spoken to like a wee laddie was punching below the belt.

Dunbar realised that some sort of power play was going on and he would have been quite happy to sit back and watch the sparks fly, but time was pressing on.

'Can I suggest we hit the road, ma'am?' he said, standing up. Stewart followed suit a few seconds later, one hand going into his pocket. Dunbar knew that the DSup's 'lucky' lighter was coming along for the ride. The only lucky thing about this trip would be for a small forest not to be burnt down.

'I agree. I want a daily report. You have my permission to give the Nightmare Man a nightmare of his own. And by that I mean locking him up in a cell, not setting fire to his hair. See yourselves out.'

SIX

Harry always got a strange feeling when he crossed the Forth into Fife. Like he was going back home again. He'd lived in Dunfermline for the best part of six years before going to university in Edinburgh, where he spent a fitful two years before joining Lothian and Borders Police.

He felt like a small child might feel running into the arms of an auntie he hadn't seen in years. Without the musty smell. It felt good to him but was also tinged with sadness, since his mother had lived in the house where Derek was living, before she died.

He tried to think happier thoughts as he drove along towards Dalgety Bay, where his brother would be waiting. If he knew what was good for him.

He listened to the radio, not hearing the tunes – they were white noise. He thought about the question

Alex had asked him recently: *What would you do if this was our last day together?*

It was a question he couldn't get out of his mind. He felt a chill run through him, as if somebody had just walked over his grave.

Alex's sister, Jessica, had come round to be with her, to spend the day with her. Jessica was the only family Alex had now after her mother and father had disowned her. All because she had married an older bloke called Harry McNeil.

Ten minutes later, the brand new pool car was turning into The Bridges, a quiet street with big houses that faced the sea and the bridges in the distance. Harry imagined what the developers were like, sitting round a large table, trying to decide what to name the street.

'Come on, Fergus, ya ginger-heided bastard! I pay you well to come up with the names, and Get It Up Ye Way just isn't cutting it.

Or maybe it was Fife Council who named the streets after the dust from the last skid steer had settled. Either way, the houses were nice, making up for the lack of imagination when it came to the street name.

Harry pulled in and Briony opened the door, as if she'd been peeping behind the curtains, waiting for him. She came down the steps, smiling at him.

'Harry!' she said as he wound the window down. 'Sorry I couldn't come along to the wee do yesterday, but I had to cover for somebody. I have some clothes and toys for Grace, and I've already spoken to Alex. We're having a girls' night in tonight, just the three of us with the wee one.'

An image of three young women getting blootered and dancing on the settee to Bruce Springsteen's 'Born in the USA' jumped into his mind. Then he reminded himself that it was he who had done that years ago at a friend's house, and the women were infinitely more responsible than he had ever been.

'That's magic. She'll be pleased to see you.'

'Heid-the-baw's coming. Just getting his jacket on,' Briony said.

'I heard that,' Derek said, walking down the pathway with a little tartan suitcase that looked barely big enough to hold a change of underwear. Then Harry saw the bag slung over his shoulder as well. Y-fronts *and* a clean vest. Harry was impressed.

'See? I told you I'd be ready,' Derek said, slipping the bag off his shoulder and opening the back door and slinging his stuff onto the back seat.

'That's because I woke him up, or else I'd be driving him down to the station now to catch the train. He said you weren't going to wait on him and I don't blame you.'

'When I said I would set an alarm, I meant Briony,' Derek said, grinning.

Harry saw a tuft of hair sticking up on the side of his brother's head as he got into the passenger seat.

'Home, James, and don't spare the horses,' Derek said.

Briony leaned into the driver's side. 'You sure about this, Harry? I mean, it's not too late to change your mind.'

'And ruin your girls' night in? I wouldn't dream of it. Besides, the Highlands are a big place. Plenty of spots to lose him.'

Briony laughed and straightened up. 'Keep him safe from the bogeyman, Harry.'

'Will do.'

He reversed out of their driveway and honked the horn as he drove away.

'Have you asked her to marry you yet?' he asked his brother.

'Now why would I want to do that?' Derek fiddled with the radio, turning the volume up a bit. 'Eighties music. You can't beat it. Not like all that mumbo jumbo shite nowadays.'

'Why would you want to do that?' Harry said, turning the sound down again. 'She's the best thing that's ever happened to you.'

Derek looked at him. 'That's my whole point: why

would I want to spoil things? Sometimes a marriage goes wrong. It's all fun and games until somebody gets an eye out. You of all people should know that.'

Harry thought about it for a moment, but he couldn't fault his brother's logic. 'If you're happy, that's the main thing.'

'I am. We are. We're doing well with the house thing. Buying them, doing them up, renting them out. It's a good wee number, Harry. You should try it.'

'We're fine just the way we are,' he replied, hitting the A921, heading back the way he had come. He'd already spoken to Jimmy Dunbar that morning, but he had held back about Derek coming. Maybe he had secretly been hoping his brother would sleep in and he would drive up on his own. No such luck.

'A few rules before we get up there,' Harry said.

'Uh-oh. Lecture time from big brother.'

'I can drop you off at the bus station in Dunfermline if you like. Let you get the lecture from the bus driver as he has to stop when you're nashing after his bus.'

'When have you ever had a bus driver stop for you? But carry on. I'm all ears.'

'Right, pay attention. I have no intention of repeating myself when we're up north. If I have to, then you're basically fucked. I will swiftly dish out a boot to the bollocks and you'll be on your own after that. Especially since DSup Stewart is going to be there. You will keep a low profile. Do your own thing during the day and we'll have dinner together. *If* the others think it's a good idea. If not, you're on your tod.'

'Aw, that's barry. Desert me miles from nowhere while there's some nut job on the loose.'

Harry looked at him for a second. 'You were the one who begged to come along.'

'I know. I'm just saying.'

'Anyway, keep your pie hole zipped. You're up there to visit our auntie and if I hear otherwise –'

Derek held up a hand. 'I know, I know. I'll be on Santa's naughty list.' He reclined the seat. 'Wake me up when we get there.'

SEVEN

'When I said we were all going to take a turn driving, I didn't actually mean I was going to get behind the wheel,' Stewart complained as they entered Inverness from the south. 'Pair of bastards.'

'I thought you were a control freak, sir?' Robbie Evans said from the back seat. 'Emphasise on the freak,' he said in a lower voice.

'Nothing wrong with wanting to be in control of your own life, son,' Stewart said, leaning forward and squinting through the windscreen. 'I mean, can you imagine burning to death in a wreck because some fucking twat couldn't drive a pig with a stick, never mind a car? I'd be well pissed-off. I mean, I'd be deid, but still. Where the fuck are we?'

'At least we're all up here in one piece, which we should be thankful for,' Jimmy Dunbar said.

Stewart looked at him and made a face. 'I hope you don't mind me saying, Jimmy, but if I'd wanted an F1 experience, I would have signed up with a driving school.'

'I do mind. I might not be Class One trained, but I can keep up with the best of them.'

'Don't talk pish.'

'Didn't your therapist tell you to relinquish some control?' Dunbar said, keeping quiet about Stewart's driving skills, or lack of them.

'God Bless Ian, but sometimes he takes things too far. I mean, look at this: we're in the car up in the Highlands on what he calls a little break. I told him I would come up so long as I was working. A wee fuckin' break. Can you see me fishing or some such nonsense?'

'I can see you with a wee tiddler, sir,' Evans said, trying not to laugh.

'Shut your fucking hole.'

'I'm glad we're coming up here in the summer again,' Evans said as they crossed over the River Ness. 'I wonder if we'll see the monster? I bet you've seen some monsters in your time.'

'What? Cheeky bastard,' Dunbar said.

'Aye, we've all had our share, son,' Stewart said, not taking his eyes off the road. 'And you'd do well to think about Linda Fry before slagging us oldies off.' He looked in the rear-view mirror. 'You were lucky she still had a pulse after shagging her. Imagine you having to explain to her family how she popped it. *Oh aye, well, I was just giving it to her and she stopped breathing, like.'*

Dunbar laughed as Evans shook his head. 'At least I'm with Vern now.'

'And you'd better be treating her right,' Dunbar said, 'or else it will be back to grab-a-granny.'

'Fuck me, this place is just as bad as driving in Edinburgh. At least there's a McDonald's.' Stewart followed the road round to the right, and they all sat and watched as the DSup pretended he knew where he was going while Evans yelled out the directions from his phone.

When they were on the Old Edinburgh Road, they knew they weren't far from their destination.

'There's the sign for Raigmore Hospital,' Dunbar said. 'We were told if we drove past that, we were on the right road.'

'And after that?'

'It's on the right.'

'I need a pish and a drink, in that order. Maybe I should have taken Flucker up on his offer to go away on my own for a wee while. This was a shite drive up here. No offence.'

Dunbar shook his head and looked out of the window as they passed the hospital entrance.

The police station was off the roundabout and

Stewart took the exit like he was foaming at the mouth. Dunbar and Evans sighed with relief when the car was parked up.

'They could have just given us one of those fucking BWM patrol cars so we could have booted it up here with the lights on. I'm going to tell the numpty who's in charge to get us one. This fucking Vauxhall is making my arse numb.'

'I'm just glad it's got airbags,' Dunbar said.

'You're still alive, though, Jimmy.'

For a police HQ, it looked pretty modern. Inside, they were greeted by a young woman who smiled at them from behind a glass-topped counter.

'How can I help you?' she said. Dunbar thought she wasn't old enough to be jaded yet, but give it time.

'We're here from Glasgow to assist in the investigation of the murder that took place last night,' Stewart said as they showed her their warrant cards.

'Oh, yes. DCI McNeil said you were expected. Come on through.'

She waved a wand and the door on their left clicked, announcing their presence. 'His name's DI Fraser. He'll be waiting for you.'

When they got through the door, a man popped his head round a door further along.

'This way, sir,' the man said.

'Lavvy first, pal,' Stewart said. 'Fucking coffee is going right through me.'

The man, who they all correctly assumed was DI Fraser, pointed to his left. 'It's along there, sir.'

Stewart walked off while the other two entered the incident room.

Harry McNeil was sitting at a desk.

'Hi, Harry,' Dunbar said and Harry got up to shake hands. 'How's the bairn?'

'She's terrific, Jimmy.' Harry shook hands with Evans. 'Good to see you again, pal.'

'You too.'

Fraser stood around like the ugly bridesmaid waiting for her first dance.

There were two other people in the room and Fraser stepped forward when the other detectives took a breath. 'This is DS Liz Aitken and DC Jack Mair.'

The younger detectives waved at the newcomers.

'You said you were going to give us a rundown on the call you received, Jimmy,' Harry said.

'I will. We'll wait for DSup Stewart to get back in.'

'Can I get you anything to drink?' Fraser asked. 'Juice from the machine?'

'Aye, go on then, pal,' Dunbar said, fishing money from his wallet to pay for the bottles, then Fraser left.

'Jesus Christ,' Stewart said, coming into the room. 'I could have put out a forest fire with that.'

That will come in handy after you take a benny and set fire to one, Dunbar thought, but kept it to himself.

'Where's that DI?' Stewart asked.

'Away to the drinks machine to get us some juice. I told him diet for you.'

'You saying I'm a fat bastard?'

'I just thought you were watching your sugar intake.'

'Listen, I might be big, but my body mass index is low. What else you got there?' he asked Fraser as the DI came back into the room. Stewart saw a regular Pepsi and pounced on it, grabbing it from the man's hand and twisting the cap off, then chugging some of it down.

'You can still have it, Jimmy,' Stewart said, 'but I backwashed some of it into the bottle.'

Choke, ya bastard. 'I'm fine, sir, thanks. I'll take the diet.'

'Suit yourself. Fat bastard.' Stewart chugged some more and let out a belch that would have melted plastic.

'Fuck me, he's started early,' Dunbar said to Harry. The resident detectives looked at each other and wondered if Stewart was on day release.

Stewart tossed the empty bottle into a nearby bin

and the lid flew somewhere close by, never to be seen again.

A young man in uniform came into the room. 'If I can get your luggage out of your cars, then I can take it to the hotel,' he said. He looked like a fifth former from a posh school, with slicked-back hair and glasses.

Dunbar and Harry gave him the keys to their pool cars.

'I'll leave the keys behind reception,' the man said, and left the room.

'Right, laddies and lassies, let's get our arses down on some chairs and we can go through what that uniform found.' Stewart looked at Fraser. 'The floor's all yours.'

Lachlan Fraser stood at the whiteboard. 'This isn't normally an incident room, being the HQ, so we had to procure' – he held up finger quotes – 'some things pending your arrival.'

Dunbar looked at the man and wondered if he was ill. He looked to be anywhere between thirty and sixty, like one of those people who go on a crash diet and end up looking like they're dying.

'You're the crew who got the shitey end of the stick,' Stewart said. 'Stuck with us hooligans from Glasgow and the posh guy from Edinburgh. Never mind, son, we'll look after you.'

Fraser looked puzzled. 'We've been on major enquiries before, sir.'

'Not saying you haven't, pal. Don't get your jock-strap in a frenzy. I meant we'll be by your side helping you. Carry on.' Stewart turned to Dunbar and said in a low voice, 'Five minutes in the place and I want to take my lighter out and burn some cunt.'

Fraser made a face, a sort of grimace that might have meant he had excessive gas from his lunch or he wasn't sure how to take Stewart. He took an envelope that was sitting on a table and pulled out some crime scene photos and stuck them on the board with magnets.

'The uniformed sergeant, Bobby McGuire, was called out to go and check the old Kirk graveyard after a call was received from your office in Glasgow. A young woman was reported missing after she had been talking with her parents on FaceTime and she thought she was being followed.'

'She was in the graveyard when she was filming?' Harry asked.

'Yes, sir. Her name was Hannah Keddie. Aged twenty-five.'

'What was she doing in the graveyard?'

'I thought DCI Dunbar could take it from here, sir. He wants to input some information.'

Dunbar stood up and walked over to a computer.

'Thanks, DI Fraser.' He looked at the others. 'Hannah Keddie was a reporter for an online magazine called Spine Chills. It's a popular thing, apparently, and they have a YouTube channel too. Hannah sometimes worked with a man on true crime. This past week, she was in town trying to catch the Nightmare Man. Unfortunately, he caught her.'

'Who's the colleague?' Harry asked.

'Guy named Eric Straw.' Dunbar turned to Fraser. 'Have you tracked him down yet?'

'No, sir.'

'Right. Straw is still missing. That makes him the main suspect. Although we're still working on motive. And I say "we" because I spoke to Hannah's parents this morning before we left. What they had to show me was a video recording. Hannah's father puts his iPhone on a little tripod and records her videos so he can watch them and give her some feedback. This time, he thought Hannah was genuinely scared. I managed, with a little help from my colleague DS Evans there, to download the video from Mr Keddie. Long story short, I got the video onto our system. I spoke to DCI McNeil this morning and explained what I needed.'

Harry nodded to him; mission accomplished. 'I got DS Aitken here to help me prepare it for viewing, and through the modern marvel we call the internet, the video is ready to play,' he said.

'A well-oiled machine, my lot,' Stewart said, as if he had personally been responsible for this achievement. 'Fucking professionals, let me tell you. But don't keep us in suspense, DCI Dunbar. Roll the fucking tape.'

They gathered round a computer screen and Liz Aitken couldn't have achieved a better effect if she was a boy wizard.

They watched sombrely as the last moments of Hannah Keddie's life played out.

EIGHT

'Where are you, honey?' Bill Keddie said to his daughter. He had propped his iPhone on the little tripod with the bendy legs on the coffee table, directly in front of the iPad they were watching the FaceTime video on. Keddie hadn't got to grips with new technology – if it didn't pour a pint, he wasn't interested – but even he had to admit how good this was.

'I'm in the old Kirk graveyard outside Muir of Ord. I was talking to a source today and he pointed me in this direction.' Hannah Keddie was out of breath, as if she had just been running before turning her phone on.

'It's dark, Hannah. I can hardly see you,' her mother, Edith, complained.

'I want to have a look around without announcing

myself,' Hannah said. 'Even though this is in the middle of nowhere.'

'Why don't you go back during daylight?' Keddie asked.

'It's more dramatic in the dark.'

'What was the tip you got?' Edith asked.

'Something to do with one of the mausoleums here. It's through in the old section.'

Her parents could see her face as she walked holding the phone towards herself. It was dark in the background, with trees and gravestones barely making an appearance. Keddie had to admit he wouldn't have had the balls to go in there at night, not without a big dog at the very least. And the blade he sometimes carried in his jacket pocket on a Friday night when he went out drinking with his pals.

They watched as their daughter flipped the picture.

Hannah walked through an archway of sorts dripping with bushes. Keddie wasn't the horticulturist in the family. Scabby bushes, he would say if anybody asked. Behind her was darkness and the wind started screeching into the microphone.

'Where's that laddie?' Keddie asked, feeling his heckles rise.

'Eric was meeting somebody who knew about the

original murders. I told him I was coming here tonight, Dad. He didn't force me. In fact, he advised against it.'

'You should have bloody listened to him. Creeping about in a graveyard after dark.'

'I want photos of the original crime scene. A girl was found in here thirty years ago. I want photos in the dark. It's going to blow the readers away.'

Hannah was smiling, then suddenly she gasped and turned round.

'What's wrong?' Keddie asked.

'Hannah, I don't think you should be there,' Edith chimed in.

'It's just the wind,' Hannah said, turning to face the camera again. Then her eyes went wide and she started to scream as the phone was snatched out of her hand. The scream intensified as the phone hit the ground and sat in long grass, staring up at the dark sky and waving tree branches.

More screams, then nothing. Until the footsteps on what was left of the gravel driveway. Then a voice whispering into the phone from out of view:

'I am Nightmare.'

There was silence in the room for a moment before Stewart stood up. He looked at Fraser. 'What did forensics have to say for themselves?'

'Due to the location, there wasn't much forensic evidence around her. The pathologist who attended said there was no indication of sexual assault. The words carved into her chest were postmortem. A shoe came off and was at the other mausoleum. He had dragged her to the one where the first victim was found thirty years ago.'

'Give us the lead-up to our getting involved,' Harry said.

'At first, the Keddies were convinced this was a prank.'

'What made them think that, son?' Dunbar said.

Fraser looked at each of the men. 'Because she had done this sort of thing in the past. She had posted something like this on her YouTube channel and then she had reappeared in the video. This time the video ended, like somebody had switched it off, and Mr Keddie thought this was the first part that had been filmed and she would edit it. It was only later on that they started getting worried. Next morning, Hannah didn't answer her phone. That's when they called us and we sent Sergeant McGuire to check on the grave-yard after uniforms visited the B&B Hannah was staying at and found her bed hadn't been slept in.'

'We heard there's been somebody spray-painting *I am Nightmare* on headstones in cemeteries around here,' Robbie Evans said.

'That's right. Three gravestones. Three different places. People are talking now, worried that the killer has come back, but up until now we were hoping it was just some teenager pranksters.'

'Looks like you were wrong,' Stewart said. He shook his head. 'A lassie was murdered, and your fucking MIT crew thought it was better to investigate the murder of an old codger.'

'It's not quite what it seems,' a voice said from the doorway. A tall woman was standing there holding the door open.

'Folks, this is –' Fraser started to say before Stewart interrupted him.

'Detective Chief Superintendent Jill Craig.'

Jill looked around the room for a moment. 'As I was saying, the *old codger*, as you put it, was retired Detective Superintendent Archie Baker. He was the lead on the original Nightmare Man case.'

NINE

Jill Craig walked to the front of the room with authority, then she turned to look at the assembled team.

'Archie Baker was one of the good guys. He was well respected and loved by everybody he worked with.' She held up a hand. 'Yes, I know that sounds like a bad obituary. But he was. That's why we have a lot of resources trying to find his killer and why we invited detectives from other divisions to help on this matter.'

'Do you think the cases are linked, ma'am?' Harry asked.

'We're not sure at the moment. I have some team members going back though Archie's old case files to see if anybody threatened him. We're also going through the old Nightmare files. Anything to see if this was a targeted killing.'

'Was there anything missing in the house?' Dunbar asked.

'Some money. Things were scattered about to make it look like a robbery, but his daughter said that he kept a filing cabinet with everything there was to know about the Nightmare Man. All those files are gone.'

'What was in those files exactly?' Stewart asked.

Jill faced him. 'His daughter said he had cut out clippings from newspapers, and he had photocopied all the files we had on Nightmare.'

'Just that case?' Evans asked.

'Yes. She doesn't know why, but she speculates that he was obsessed because Nightmare was the one that got away, as it were. Her father refused to talk about it.'

'If you don't mind, ma'am, I'd like to send one of my team along with one of yours, just so we can get up to speed,' Stewart said.

'Fine. We can liaise. I'm leading the team on the Baker case. We'll have a briefing at the end of the day.' They swapped phone numbers. 'Call me later.'

'Will do.'

'Right, nice meeting you all, and we'll be seeing a lot of each other no doubt.' Jill Craig left the room.

'Right, now I need somebody to go and have a word with the pathologist at the mortuary,' Stewart said to Fraser. 'Which is where?'

'Raigmore.'

'Right. DS Aitken, you're on point. Get us a pool car and then you can drive us around. I want us to see the crime scene for ourselves. Then I want to go to the mortuary. Then we can have Baker's daughter into the station to interview her.'

'Yes, sir,' Liz said, picking up a phone.

Stewart turned to Fraser. 'Get them to keep trying to find this Straw bloke. He's a priority.'

'Yes, sir.'

'Mair. You stay with the uniforms and get everything up on the whiteboard. If we think we need more bodies in here, I'll talk to DCS Craig. Everybody get to it.'

Liz hung up the phone. 'There's a car waiting for us.'

'No' a fucking Mini, I hope.'

'More like a maxi.'

'Good job. You can drive.'

TEN

'Just so you know, trust is a two-way street,' Stewart shouted from the back of the minibus.

Dunbar grinned from the front seat. 'Big bairn was expecting a jam sandwich BMW.'

'I heard that.' Stewart slumped back in his seat, fidgeting to get his legs stretched out. 'Fucking bus indeed.'

'At least we're getting driven around, sir,' Evans said.

'Aye, at least we don't have to shite ourselves because you're behind the wheel. You look like you're in a fucking trance when you're driving. Small mercies we got here in one piece. You're doing no' bad there, hen!' Stewart shouted to Liz.

'Ignoramus,' Dunbar said in a low voice, and Liz giggled.

'I hope you're no' talking about me up there, Jimmy?'

'I thought you weren't deef?' Evans said.

'Shut your fucking pie hole.' Stewart looked to the other side of the minibus. 'You're quiet now, Harry. Everything alright there, son?'

Harry turned round to look at the boss. 'Fine, sir. Just miles away. I'm thinking about the bairn back home.'

'Aye, you miss them when they're that age. My daughter has a wee yin and luckily that fuckin' old boot of an ex-wife hasn't poisoned her against me. Not for a lack of trying, though, but what she didn't take into account is, Claire is a daddy's girl.'

'Remember that even though Chance is eighteen now, he's still your bairn too,' Jimmy said.

'I won't forget, Jimmy.'

Liz was driving them back the way they had come. The van was hot inside after sitting in the June sunshine, but the windows in the front had been rolled down pretty sharpish and now Harry was feeling the breeze on his face.

He hadn't been thinking about Grace at all. He had been thinking about his dad, a Northern Constabulary police officer years before they had become a unified police force.

His dad, George McNeil, hadn't spoken about his

work much. Now and again, when he'd one too many whiskies, he would rattle on about what a shower of bastards people were, about how he dealt with the dregs in life, but he forgot to mention the good he had done while in uniform. He'd saved a child drowning in a river. Done CPR on a dying man in the street whose heart had decided to give up at that point.

Even when he moved to CID, he had done a lot of good, but George was the ultimate pessimist. Glass half empty all the time.

One thing in particular Harry remembered was his father talking about the Nightmare Man. Yes, his mother had threatened the kids with a visit from a non-existent entity, until that very same entity had sprung to life.

It had been a worry for them all at the time. He remembered talking to his dad about it, or trying to, but George had said it was something he couldn't talk about.

The minibus shoogled side to side as they raced up the hill outside Muir of Ord. The hills in the distance looked spectacular in the sun. Harry always felt at peace coming here, and the thought of his dad made him think of his mother, now in her grave.

They'd had good times playing up in Inverness. Their street had been a quiet one, and he, Derek and Mel had plenty of friends. Staying out late in the summer holidays had been fun. Until the nightmare that haunted their waking hours.

Harry remembered spending a lot of time indoors after the killings. His mother had warned him well to stay beside his siblings. They had to go everywhere together.

'With a bit of imagination, this could be a Hollywood tour bus,' Evans said.

'If you're going to continue to talk shite, you'll be walking back,' Stewart shouted. 'Fucking Hollywood. There are just as many heid-the-baws there as there are in Holyrood. Same shite, different town, if you ask me.'

Dunbar turned to look at Evans, silently telling him to shut his hole.

At the top of the hill, where Sergeant Bobby McGuire was sure he'd heard a distant voice telling him to just lie down and things would be so much better on the other side, Liz turned left, taking the same route as old Tam had taken in his Morris Minor.

'How come this church is so out of the way?' Stewart asked as the van raced downhill before shooting up the other side. 'Fuck me, it's like a roller coaster.'

'It was a small church for the village further on. People from down the road started coming too, but it soon got too small and they built a bigger one down in the town when the population rose,' Liz said.

She drove a little further on and they saw the patrol car parked outside the graveyard. Liz wound a window down and spoke to the uniform who was standing guard, and he directed her to park behind the other vehicles round the corner.

They drove past the old church, which looked like it had escaped from the set of a horror film.

'You said that Hannah Keddie came from Glasgow?' Harry said.

'Originally,' Dunbar answered.

'Did she have a boyfriend?'

'Not according to them. Her colleague Eric Straw lived up here and he gave her some flannel about how life was so much better up here. She fell for it and made the move.'

'Flannel, sir?' Liz said, taking her eyes off the track for a moment.

'Eyes on the road,' Stewart shouted from the back. 'We don't want our names carved on one of those fucking things just yet.'

'You know what I mean,' Dunbar said in his own defence. 'The grass is always greener and all that.'

'Well, we've been unable to establish his residence. Just because we can't get hold of him, doesn't meant to say he's on the run,' Liz replied, parking behind a patrol car. Forensics vehicles were further ahead.

'He's got to live somewhere.'

They piled out into the long grass that bordered the rough track.

'Seems like the council couldn't give a shit about keeping places like these in some kind of order,' Stewart complained.

'They don't have enough resources to go around cutting old, abandoned graveyards,' Liz said.

'Obviously you haven't been around as long as I have, Sergeant. If this was Glasgow or Edinburgh, they'd have a block of flats built on this place by now.'

'At least the gravestones haven't been tipped over,' Harry said.

They walked through the archway in the stone wall after another uniform showed them the way. When they were through, the sun slipped behind some clouds that had formed into a gang, making the scene more ominous.

'How up to speed are you on the original murders?' Harry asked Liz.

'We've been reading up on them ever since Hannah Keddie was found yesterday, but we'd appreciate somebody filling in the blanks.'

'Go on then,' Stewart urged. 'Give us the spooky tour of this place.'

'Around thirty years ago, three victims were found, a few days apart, in the graveyard. All of them had been murdered. All of them had *I am Nightmare* carved on their chests.'

'Same MO as our current victim?' Harry asked.

'Yes. Same place, same exact location within the graveyard. There was one difference, though: all of the previous victims had had one of their little fingers cut off.'

Harry and Dunbar looked at each other for a moment. 'A finger?' Harry said.

'Yes. Each finger had been cut off cleanly, like with a sharp knife. Something like that, the pathologist at the time said.'

'What about Hannah Keddie?' Dunbar asked.

'I'm not sure. DI Fraser saw the body, and I was busy with uniforms trying to get them to check the nearest premises to see if anybody had seen anything unusual.'

'What about the sergeant who found her? What's his name again?' Stewart asked.

'McGuire. I don't know, sir.'

'Well, find out, for fuck's sake. That's not the sort of thing you miss.'

'Yes, sir. I'll call DI Fraser right now.' Her cheeks had started to go red as she walked out of the way and took her phone out to call the boss.

A forensics tent had been placed over the scene where the victim had been found. It was next to an old stone mausoleum, ornately carved with a wrought-iron gate at the front.

Harry looked at the front of the white stone building, now drab with dirt. He wondered why the mausoleums were here, in an out-of-the-way place.

Then he looked at the mantle above the doorway and he froze for a moment. Harris.

The killer whom the press had named the Tattoo Artist hadn't killed up here near Inverness as far as they knew, but had struck down in Edinburgh. But here was a connection: this graveyard where young women were found murdered with a finger cut off, and Colin Harris, who had been convicted and given a life sentence and who had cut off the fingers of his victims. As it turned out, Colin Harris hadn't been working alone, and they had only recently caught his partner.

'See the name there?' he said to Dunbar. 'I wonder if Colin Harris was a relative.'

'We can find out. When we get to the station, we'll make sure somebody finds that out.'

A wind blew the trees and the undergrowth.

A man in a white suit approached them. 'Jerry White, head of forensics.' White was a big man, almost as big as Stewart, and he had a far better demeanour.

'You're not a friend of O'Toole's, are you?' Stewart said, ready to have a fight.

'Who?'

'Never mind. Get us up to speed, son.'

'Yes, sir. Well, the victim was murdered here. There's blood soaked into the ground and spatter on the side of the mausoleum. We've tried taking prints from the side of the stone wall, but there's nothing there. This was rage, pure and simple. I've seen it before at a domestic when the husband stabbed the wife thirty-seven times. The pathologist said this girl was stabbed ten times. In my experience, that's overkill.'

'Agreed,' Harry said. 'We're trying to locate a colleague of hers now.'

'Have you ever heard of a website called Spine Chills?' Evans asked White.

White turned to look at him. 'I have actually. I thought I recognised the name when we got the call. It's pretty good. They have a YouTube channel, they do podcasts. It's quite popular. I like it because I work with real crime.'

'You know of Eric Straw then?'

'Yes, of course. He's quite the celebrity around here. Especially since he lives along in the next town. And when Hannah Keddie came up to work here, a lot of people were happy. They have a big following.'

Dunbar looked puzzled. 'Wait; I thought she lived in Glasgow?'

'She did. But then she announced she was moving

up here to be with her boyfriend.'

'Boyfriend?' Stewart said. 'Nobody told us about a fucking boyfriend.'

'They did a podcast about it,' White explained. '*Everybody* knew there was a big age difference between her and Eric Straw, but most people thought it was great. But haters are going to hate. They got some nasty comments.'

'Like what?' Harry asked.

'Oh, you know, the usual. *Fuck off and die, slut.* That sort of thing. *Cradle snatcher, beast, pervert.* Some people can't help themselves.'

'I think we need to have a look at this channel,' Dunbar said.

'They made it quite public on one of the podcasts. About the hatred, I mean. Eric was upset, but he took it on the chin. He loved Hannah, he said, and nobody was going to put him off.'

'Any animosity between them?' Dunbar asked.

'Not that anybody knew. Hannah didn't mention anything like that on her site or in her podcasts.'

Liz came back. She looked sombre. 'I spoke to DI Fraser. He said there was a finger missing.'

'Jesus,' Stewart said. 'Thanks, Jerry.'

'No problem, sir.' White turned and walked back to the forensics tent.

'See? That's how a forensics man should talk to a

superior officer, no' like that wee sheep-shaggin' bastard back in Glasgow. I wouldn't promote him to head of toilet cleaning services, never mind fucking forensics. He'd better keep out of my way or the only thing he'll be shoving a microscope up is his own arse.'

'To the mortuary?' Dunbar said, thinking that was a place Stewart would end up if he kept on with his ranting.

'Aye. And I'll call Jill Craig so we can double the effort to find that piece of shit Straw. He has to be hiding somewhere.'

'It's early days, sir. We're trying to locate family in the area,' Liz said. 'Unless he managed to snag a room with a friend. We're still doing background checks on him.'

They walked back to the minibus and Stewart climbed in, his weight bending it to one side alarmingly. 'I think the springs are shot on this thing,' he said, bouncing down into a seat.

'Nothing to do with him being a fat bastard,' Evans said to Dunbar.

'I fucking heard that,' Stewart said. 'You're the only bastard who'll be bringing his wallet out in the bar tonight for that remark.'

'Fuck me,' Evans said.

Harry laughed. 'You should speak more quietly, son.'

ELEVEN

They drove back through Inverness and headed for Raigmore Hospital.

'I can feel my guts going just thinking about this place,' Harry complained.

'I didn't take you for a Jessie,' Stewart said from his reserved spot at the back of the minibus.

'I've never been able to stand the smell,' Harry said. 'Bodies I can deal with. The smell makes me boak every time. I don't know what it is.'

'Seriously? Fuck me. I can eat a good hearty breakfast afterwards.'

'Jesus, please don't talk about food.'

Stewart laughed. 'Tell you what, mucker, you and Liz go and get a coffee at the restaurant. Me, Jimmy and that wee deviant will go and have a look at the victim. And don't say Uncle Calvin isn't good to you. But if you don't put your hand in your wallet tonight, I'll write your name on the lavvy wall back at the station. *Harry McNeil pissed his pants in the mortuary.*'

'Drinks are on me then,' Harry replied.

'And heid-the-baw there. Evans isn't married and lives with his old ma, fucking sponging off her. He's loaded. I'd better see that wallet opening and closing so fast he gets friction burns.'

Liz pulled into a tight space, but nobody gave a crap if a beat-up old minibus from Police Scotland got a few more dings. No matter where they parked, even in the middle of a field, some stupid bastard would park right next to them.

'Right, boys and girls. Let's get out into the fresh air. I'm sure that manky wee bastard let one go earlier. Fucking bus is stinking.'

'I didn't let one go,' Evans said. 'Whoever smelt it, dealt it.'

Stewart laughed. 'Listen, son, if I farted in this heap o' shite, you'd fucking know it. Now get oot.'

They made their way to the main entrance and Liz and Harry went to the restaurant, while the other three made it to the mortuary.

The pathologist was a young man with glasses and a cheery smile, more akin to a bank manager who was about to ream you for putting your account into overdraft.

'Welcome,' he said. 'I'm Dr Ed Corvin.'

'You know why we're here,' Stewart said, taking an instant dislike to the man. He reminded him of Ian Flucker. Which wasn't a bad thing in itself, but Flucker had power and that was something that stuck in Stewart's throat.

'I do indeed. She's waiting for you through here.'

'Like we're here to take her to a dance,' Dunbar said as the pathologist walked through a set of rubber doors.

'Evans would be lucky to take a corpse to a dance,' Stewart whispered.

'I'm right here,' Evans said.

'And?' Stewart said, looking at him.

'I have a girlfriend. Vern and I are still seeing each other.'

'Good for you, son. Is that what you're calling your blow-up doll these days?'

They followed the doctor through and the smell of the place hit them. Disinfectant with a hint of lingering death.

They walked through to the refrigeration room and an assistant pulled open a drawer. Hannah Keddie was lying under a sheet, only her head showing.

'I did the PM earlier. She was quite healthy, to be

honest. Cause of death was a sharp instrument dissecting the carotid in her neck. Death would have taken no more than a couple of minutes.'

'What was the time of death?' Dunbar asked.

'Around eleven p.m. to midnight, Thursday night.'

Dunbar looked at Stewart. 'Right about the time she was doing the live stream with her folks.'

'Finger missing?' Evans asked.

'Funny you should ask,' Corvin said, pulling the sheet back gently. They could see the little finger was missing. And there were bruises on her arms. Fresh ones.

'Maybe domestic abuse from this Straw guy?' Dunbar said.

Corvin gently lifted her left hand, turning it over. On the little finger was roughly tattooed the number 1.

'Fuck me,' Dunbar said, looking at Stewart.

'You worked the case with McNeil in Edinburgh and the Tattoo Artist had an accomplice we didn't know about at first. He died, yet here we are with some other bastard doing it. Copycat or somebody else we didn't know about?'

Stewart left the question hanging.

'How long have you been in MIT?' Harry asked, blowing on the hot cup of coffee.

Liz sat opposite him with a cup of tea. 'Almost a year. I was in CID for a while, and I applied for MIT but had to wait for an opening. It would have gone quicker in a bigger city, I suppose, but I'm here now.'

'I suppose a lot of people don't think there's much crime up here,' Harry said, thinking of the comments his brother had made.

'You'd be surprised.' She looked at him with a smile. 'You seriously don't like the smell of the mortuary?'

'Don't you start. I get enough slagging off my wife. She's a detective too.'

'Really. Do you work with each other?'

'Yes, she's MIT as well. She's just ending her maternity leave. We had a baby girl. I have an older son, Chance. He's eighteen and joined the force too.'

'Keeping it in the family.'

'Indeed.' He looked at her. 'Jerry White seems to be a big fan of Hannah Keddie.'

'Yes. He joins us in the pub. He's a great laugh, to be honest. He's got a great personality, and he's a big fan of true crime. It's what got him into working in forensics, he says.'

'Are you a fan of the online true crime podcasts?'

'No, I'm a fan of comedy reruns. From the nineties

especially. *Friends* and shows like that. I like something that can make me laugh. Or somebody.'

'How old are you, if you don't mind me asking? Or does that go against some HR rule?'

She laughed. 'Harry, you can ask me anything you like. I'm thirty-five. Thirty-six in September. I like a man with a sense of humour and long walks on the beach. How does that sound for a dating website profile?'

'If it was me, long walks on the beach would be too much exercise.'

'I don't have a man in my life, but I'm not at the website thing just yet.'

'I'm in my forties and I find that would be the only way forward if my wife left me.'

He felt the presence behind him before he saw Stewart. 'That's not the way forward for me, Harry, son. I'm out and about, giving it the biscuit on the dance floor. You're only as old as you feel. Jesus, you're a good ten years younger than me and look at you: you're like an old dishcloth that needs wrung out. All this divorce shite has made me a new man. I have to fight the women off with a stick.'

'They fight him off by holding up a cross,' Evans said to Dunbar.

'I'm no' deef, bawbag.' Stewart looked at Evans and slowly shook his head. 'By the time you've finished keeping us in drink, you'll be taking out a mortgage.' Then to Liz: 'How about coming out for a drink and showing us around some of the better haunts?'

'I might just do that. You coming along, Harry?' Liz looked expectantly at him.

'Sure. Why not? Inverness on a Saturday night. What else is there to do?'

'Right then, let's get back to the station. It seems like our elusive Mr Straw is a wife beater as well. I want to get in his face and ask him if he wants to grab me by the arms and bruise me. And by fuck, I hope he tries it. I've not booted some bastard in the bollocks for a long time.' Stewart turned to Evans. 'Keep that in mind every time you want to run off your mouth.'

TWELVE

The station was hot and sweaty, not unlike the Bangkok whorehouse that Lynn McKenzie had talked of.

'Don't get him riled-up,' Dunbar warned Evans.

'I wasn't riling him. Just pointing out some truths.'

'Truths, riled-up, same fucking diff. Just keep your bloody mouth shut. It's bad enough when the big radge goes off on a tangent without you poking him with a stick.'

'That's the only poke he'll get.'

'There you again,' Dunbar said. 'You can't fucking help yourself. Stop trying to make my life a misery. If he jumps all over me, you're fucking next.'

They made it into the conference room / incident room / Christmas party snogging room. Fraser had a window open, letting in warm air and traffic noise. A couple of fans were belting out a tune that only dogs would understand.

'Keep that door open,' Stewart barked at a uniform. 'Get a cross-breeze in. From one former fat bastard to a current fat bastard, we always need fans on, even in the winter.' He nodded to Fraser, who looked around to see if Stewart was confusing him with somebody else, but no, the DSup meant him.

'That's a good idea,' Fraser said. Harry wondered if the younger detective was anorexic. Or a drinker. He'd known plenty of blokes who were thin and big drinkers.

'Right, we discovered that there's a pretty good chance that Eric Straw was an abuser. Hannah has bruising on her arm where she was forcibly grabbed,' Stewart said. 'She also had a finger cut off and the number one tattooed on her other little finger. Like how the Tattoo Artist operated. How are we on tracing this Straw wanker?'

'I had Jack look through the website for the Spine Chills magazine and Straw is there. The thing is, there's no listing for him anywhere. It might be an alias,' Fraser said. 'When we did a Google search, that's all his name comes up in.'

'No shit. What fucking genius said that was a real name?'

'It's just that he's famous,' Mair said.

'Did you ever get his autograph, son?'

'No, sir.'

'Sounds like this Straw twat rides the Loch Ness monster to work. Have you ever actually seen him?'

'Not in the flesh,' Mair answered.

'Photos then, right? You've seen photos of him.'

'Not exactly.'

'What does that mean?' Harry said. 'You have or you haven't.'

Mair drew in a breath, as if what he was about to say was on a par with admitting his sighting of the monster was utterly made-up shite. 'You see, his photo on the website is a guy standing with a raincoat and big hat on. Like a stock photo.'

'Show me,' Stewart said.

Mair tutted as if being questioned about it wasn't bad enough, but now he had to show the teacher that the dog really did eat his homework.

'There you go,' he said, pushing back his office chair with a little too much gusto, in a *fuck you* way that Stewart didn't fail to notice.

They looked at the screen and Mair was right enough: it was a night shot and Eric Straw was wearing a grey raincoat and a fedora. His face was in complete shadow.

'Right, so that's a no-go,' Stewart said, turning to Dunbar. 'Jimmy, get on the phone and call Hannah

Keddie's parents. Ask them why they didn't tell you their daughter had moved up here.'

Dunbar got up and walked out of the room, taking his phone out. He called the Keddies.

'Mrs Keddie? This is DCI Dunbar, Police Scotland. I have a question for you: when we spoke about your daughter, you failed to mention that she had moved up here to be with her boyfriend.'

'She didn't have a boyfriend.'

'That's not what she said on her website. Or podcasts, whatever.'

'If she did, then she never told us. She wanted a change of scenery.'

'How long ago did she move up here?'

'A week ago.'

'And she never mentioned any man in her life.'

'I have to go,' Mrs Keddie said abruptly and hung up. Alarm bells went off in Dunbar's mind. He walked back into the incident room and ushered Evans over. 'Call the mortuary and ask the pathologist how old he thinks those bruises are.'

'Right on it.'

Evans left and walked into the corridor. Their own incident room back in Glasgow was big enough for you to find a quiet corner to make a call or, failing that, an empty office. The corridor in this HQ was an extension of their makeshift incident room.

'Dr White? It's DS Evans. I'd like to ask you a question.'

'Fire away, but bear in mind, I haven't actually seen the monster itself.'

'I'm sorry?'

'People who come up here ask if the monster is real.'

'Can you determine how old the bruises on Hannah Keddie's arm are?'

'A few days old at the most.'

'Thanks, Doctor.' Evans cut the call and went back into the room. The change in temperature was noticeable, and he was glad the door had been jammed open. He relayed his findings to Dunbar.

'What are you thinking, sir?' he asked.

'I'm wondering if she came up here and didn't realise she was getting into an abusive relationship.'

'She made such a song and dance about her move on her website,' Harry said. He looked at Evans. 'Have you ever seen this Eric Straw on the YouTube channel?'

Evans shook his head. 'No, it's always Hannah. Straw was always listed as a contributor, and he mainly wrote on the website.'

Harry looked at Dunbar. 'I'm beginning to think this Straw bloke doesn't exist.'

'Just a made-up character on the website?'

'Why would she do that?' Evans asked.

'Maybe for security,' Harry answered. 'So people would think there was always a man around.'

'Which would make sense if somebody else was physically abusing her,' Dunbar said. 'Like her father. It might put him off coming up here if he knew she had a male friend here to protect her.'

'He sounded protective on that video,' Evans countered.

'Could be all for show, that, son.'

Stewart walked across to them. 'It's been a long day, but I want you three to go and have a scout around Hannah Keddie's room at the B&B. Forensics will be crawling all over it, but maybe you'll find an old curtain twitcher who saw something.' He turned to look at the others. 'By the looks of this lot, they couldn't light a fart with a blowtorch.'

'You staying here, sir?'

'Aye. I want to hear about the original murders. Archie Baker's daughter is coming in. I want to talk to her. I'll meet you at the hotel in, say' – he looked at his watch – 'an hour. Hour and a half tops. I hope that glaikit fuck with the glasses took our cases to the right hotel, or else we might be bunking with each other in a fucking tent.'

'I'd shoot myself first,' Dunbar said.

'Aye, it would be a bit of a tight squeeze, right enough,' Harry said.

'I have a feeling that the Thistle Hotel is some-body's idea of a joke,' Evans said. 'It isn't preceded by the word Hyatt or Holiday Inn.'

'Don't use big words, Robbie,' Dunbar said. 'You'll only trip yourself up.'

'Exponentially.'

'Shut the fuck up and get us the keys for the minibus.'

THIRTEEN

'Thanks for coming in, Miss Baker,' Stewart said, after introducing himself and DI Lachlan Fraser.

'Call me Susan,' she said, dabbing at her eyes with a paper hankie. She looked to be in her forties, but the swollen eyes and puffy cheeks could have added another ten years.

'Susan. Okay. I know this is hard for you, but can you give us a wee bit more background into why your dad kept all the Nightmare Man stuff?'

'He worked on the original murders, and it became an obsession. He lived and breathed that case. It was one he never solved. It ate away at him. It was awful to see that case get such a grip on him. For fifteen years it consumed him. Then he retired and it still consumed him. My mother died and he mourned her passing, but then it was all about that case. Some men take up bowling or golf, but not my dad. His hobby was trying to solve a fifteen-year-old cold case. It became his hobby for the next fifteen years.'

'The forensics team were looking at the house and found no signs of forced entry,' Fraser said.

'Not surprising. My dad never locked his front door. Ironic, isn't it: chasing a killer for all those years, yet he never locked his front door. You would think that he would be overcautious, but one day he said to me, if that bastard comes in here, he'll be leaving in a body bag. I think he was wrong. Stubborn old fool.'

'Had he had any threatening letters recently? Weird phone calls? Anything like that?'

'Threatening letters? Not that he mentioned to me. I don't know why somebody would threaten him. He was mostly harmless. He complained a lot, but I never heard anybody say a bad word about him.'

'Do you know what was in his files?' Stewart asked. 'Like, what sort of things he kept regarding the case?'

'Old reports he'd had copied. Newspaper clippings. Stories from rag magazines, as he called them. You know the sort of thing: Elvis lives at the South Pole. Sensationalist stuff. Every now and again, they would do an article on the Nightmare Man. I think it was because it was such an urban myth and people were bringing him to life. Then somebody really did bring him to life, and that lassie got in touch with Dad. Wanting to do an interview.'

'Hannah Keddie?'

'Aye, that's her. He was excited. It gave him a new lease of life. She said she had been sent an anonymous tip via her website that somebody was spray-painting *I am Nightmare* on gravestones in Inverness.'

'Did your dad know Hannah before that?'

'Oh aye. They used to live up here, the Keddies. He was a police officer.'

Stewart looked at her. 'Did Keddie work with your dad?'

'He did. He hadn't been long in CID when the murders happened. He stayed in the force for about five years after that. My dad talked about nothing else. All the others on the team too. Willie Dowd, George McNeil and Robert Briggs. And that psycho Jeremy Wilson, he was the force psychologist. Nobody liked him around here. He was creepy. Him and his weird friend.'

'What weird friend?'

'I can't remember that family's name. They had a wee girl, but not long after the killings, they moved. I remember my mum was upset because she and the wife were friends. It was the father who was weird. Or maybe he was just strict or something. Anyway, they moved away from the area. The man was a police officer, but he left the force and was moving to take up a new job. Oh, what was their name again? God, I can't remember.'

'Did your dad have an opinion of this other officer?' Fraser asked.

'He didn't like him. My dad had a tight-knit team. He felt this other bloke wasn't part of the team. He wasn't exactly a loner, but he just didn't click with the others.'

'Did your dad keep any notebooks with names in it or anything like that?' Stewart asked. 'Maybe giving an opinion on who he thought the Nightmare Man might have been?'

'He might have, but I didn't see anything like that. But he didn't like Jeremy Wilson, that was for sure. He thought the man was cocky. I remember my dad telling me a story from not that long ago. He said one day he and Wilson were talking, and Wilson bragged that he could get away with anything.'

'What did he mean by that?' Stewart asked.

'My dad thought Wilson meant he could get away with murder.'

FOURTEEN

It turned out that Eric Straw *did* exist after all. According to Miss Marple of the Oakwood Guest House. The B&B was situated in the southwest of the city, near a SPAR and, if your legs were up for a good stroll, a Tesco.

'Oh, no, I don't allow people to bring their own food in. If I did, the next thing you know, there's some fatso tourist honking out my bedroom. Well, not *my* bedroom, you understand.'

Harry guessed the woman was aged between forty and sixty, depending on which way the wind was blowing. Her hair was cut short, obviously coloured with the help of a bottle, and was not dissimilar to the fur of the Scotty dog she was holding under one arm.

'I know this is difficult, Mrs...?' Dunbar said. They were on the doorstep of the house and another tech brushed by them uttering something under his mask, which could either have been *thank you* or *fuck you*, Harry wasn't quite sure.

'Campbell. Isla Campbell. Mrs Campbell to you. I know what you big city slickers from Glasgow are like. One minute all smiles, just like a shark; next thing I know, my bed sheets are gone. Bloody towels too.'

They were outside the guest house where Hannah Keddie had checked in a week ago. The sun was shining down on them now, and Harry could feel his mouth getting parched and he was sweating in places he hadn't known existed until five minutes ago.

'I can assure you we're not here to steal your towels,' Harry said. Since he was from Edinburgh, he could only speak for himself, but he was reasonably sure that if Jimmy Dunbar wanted towels, he wouldn't target a place like this.

'I rent out five rooms, you know. I mean, God rest that lassie's soul and all that, but she looked the sort who would pinch towels.'

'How long was she here for?' Dunbar asked.

'She was booked in for two weeks and stayed five nights.' The dog looked up at her for a moment as if to agree. 'I turned people away because I thought she was coming back. Her stuff was here.'

'She didn't give any indication of where she was going?'

'She just said she was meeting her boyfriend.'

They all perked up at that. 'Boyfriend?' Dunbar said.

'Yes. Eric Straw. She sat and told me all about him over a cup of tea. See, that's what's disappointing: she was a nice girl. I can't say I approve of how she made a living, but at least she kept her clothes on. There are worse ways to make money. Personally, I couldn't see how she made money at all, but she did. And she was smitten with this Straw man. He was some online writer too, and she had been talking to him for a while, and he was asking her to come up here and live, but she had been hesitant. It was the Nightmare Man who made her come up, she said. After Straw told her about the grave-stones being vandalised. She saw this as an opportunity not only to make money but to start a new life.'

'Did you meet Straw?' Evans said.

'No, but I did see her get into a car further along the road on Sunday night. Somebody was driving it and she got in the passenger side and it turned around and made off.'

'Did you get the number plate of the car?' Harry said.

The woman raised her eyes and looked at him before answering. 'God bless you, son, for thinking that I'm young enough to still have telescopic eyesight, but alas, unless I was lying under the car with my head two inches from the plate, then I would have to say, not on this occasion.'

'Make and model?' Evans asked hopefully.

This time, Isla looked at him like he was really taking the piss. 'If it was a Rolls-Royce and it was sitting outside my front door, then maybe, but since it wasn't, I'm going to have to pass on that.'

'Colour?' Harry said. *Give us something, for fuck's sake.*

'It was dark. The car was dark.'

'Right, this was on Sunday night. When did she check in?' Dunbar asked.

'She checked in Saturday afternoon. She met him Sunday night. She was around on Monday evening. I saw her get into that car again on Monday night. I didn't see her on Tuesday. Saw her on Wednesday when we had a wee cuppa and a chat about her magazine and things. And her boyfriend. I assumed that was who she was getting into the car with. I told her he could come here and pick her up, but she said, "It's complicated." I thought then that he was a married man.'

'When was the actual time you last saw her?' Harry asked.

'Thursday before dinner. She was sitting in the

lounge with some drawings on a pad. That's one thing she left behind.'

'Can we have a look at it?'

'Listen, son, you're out here because your lot has turned my guest house into an episode of *Dixon of Dock Green*. I can barely get Mitzy in for her dinner. The other guests will have to forgo dinner tonight. That will please Mr Langston and his *fiancée*.' Finger quotes. 'He's been planning his nuptials for ten years. Every summer he brings a new one. He's ordered more cakes than I have. He gets older, but his fiancées stay the same age. He owns his own business, you know. Loaded. But I'm not one to gossip.'

'Do you still have the drawing pad?' Harry said, and then another forensics officer came out and this one pulled his face mask down. Jerry White.

'Hello, boys.' He smiled at them. 'Your boss had enough for the day?'

'Not exactly,' Dunbar said. 'He's back at the station.'

'Ah, right.' White winked at Dunbar behind Isla's back and nodded at the back of her head.

'If you'll excuse us,' Harry said. The three detectives walked further into the little car park and huddled round White. Harry saw Isla head back indoors with a tut. Juicy gossip opportunity out the window.

'We checked Hannah Keddie's room. We've dusted for prints, but if Mrs Campbell says there was nobody else in there, then we won't find anything. Unless Hannah sneaked somebody in.'

'Hannah got into a car further along the road, so I'd guess she didn't have anybody in the room.'

'We'll probably have a lot of prints, but more than likely they'll be from previous guests. We went through her belongings, but there wasn't much. Not even a laptop, which would have been expected since her whole life was online. Maybe she took it with her when she met that guy in the car.'

'She probably did. Some people upload stuff right away,' Harry said. 'Did you find a drawing pad by any chance?'

'No, there was nothing like that.'

'Thanks, Jerry,' Dunbar said. The forensics man nodded and walked away.

'Hannah worked with this guy Straw, who doesn't seem to exist except online, but we know she got into a car with somebody,' Harry said. 'There's a good chance that was her killer. We need to get an IP address for the magazine and the podcasts. See if we can track him that way.'

'I'll have that Mair laddie get on it back at the station,' Evans said. 'He looks a bit of a geek.'

'I noticed Hannah was left beside a Harris family mausoleum,' Harry said.

'I noticed that,' Dunbar replied. 'Harris was cremated, wasn't he?'

Harry shook his head. 'No. He was buried in that cemetery. In a dingy corner with a small marker. The family didn't want him put in the family crypt.'

'Did he have any family of his own?' Evans asked.

'He wasn't married and he didn't have any kids. His mother was still alive when he was caught, but she died. We got notice. She was cremated.'

'Who arranged the funeral?' Dunbar said.

'I don't know, but we can find out. We'll pull the death certificate and see who registered it.' Harry looked at his watch. 'Time we called it a day, don't you think? Stewart will be eating a pair of curtains if we're late getting to the hotel.'

'Aye. We'll start fresh in the morning.' Dunbar looked at Evans. 'Try and keep it together tonight, son. Stewart's bad enough when he's sober, but we know what he's like when he's pished.'

'Aye-aye, Captain.'

FIFTEEN

Stewart called Dunbar and said he was on the way but couldn't find the hotel. After Dunbar made an enquiry, he called Stewart back and gave him the bad news.

'The Thistle Hotel isn't in Inverness.'

'Where the fuck is it then?'

By Stewart's tone, Dunbar figured the older detective was having a guess and was going to be proven right.

'Muir of Ord.' Dunbar grinned at Harry and put the phone on speaker.

'Aw fuckin' hell. When I speak to that sheep-shaggin' bastard in the office when we get back, he'll think his arsehole's been bitten by a fuckin' badger, I'll plant my boot so far up his fuckin' arse. They should have had the usual wee lassie doin' it. Why did they get that fuckin' gawk to do it? Jesus fuckin' wept.'

Harry smiled and shook his head.

'Tell me they've got a bar.'

'There's one across the road.'

'Och away and have a fuckin' word wi' yersel. I'm going to nut that wee fuck when we get back.' Silence for a moment and Dunbar thought Stewart was setting fire to the new pool car. Maybe they should have stuck with the minibus.

'Right, fuck off and let me get up the road. I could eat a scabby horse.'

Stewart disconnected the call and Evans hit the A9 and then the A832 to the small town. A fifteen-minute drive, unless you were driving angry like Stewart, then ten minutes tops, and Dunbar hoped that nobody got into a road rage fight with him.

The drive was uneventful, with the sun still high, making its way to close of business.

The hotel looked like a Victorian granite house with well-kept gardens and a big enough car park. When Evans pulled into the car park, Stewart was already out of his car, flicking his lighter. He was talking on his phone.

'Aye, of course I'm taking it easy, Ian. Swearing? Me? Give over. I've turned over a new leaf. No stress, no shouting or swearing. Just getting my head down with the other lads and lassies. Aye, no problem. Talk to you then.'

He hung up as the others stood looking at him.

'What?' he said. 'I've mostly cut out the swearing. That was me checking in with Ian Flucker, the force psychologist. Nice bloke but wet behind the ears. You know the secret to getting on in life? Tell the fucks what they want to hear.'

'Can't fault that logic,' Harry agreed.

'Look at this place,' Stewart said, nodding to the building. 'Looks like the big fuckin' hoose in the *Psycho* film.'

The front door opened and a man walked out.

'Look, here's fucking Norman now.'

'Good evening, gentlemen!' the man said, all smiles and bonhomie. If he had heard Stewart's description of the property, he was ignoring it and putting on a brave face. 'I'm Harvey Shipley.'

'We're with Police Scotland,' Dunbar said.

'Yes, I know. The young man who brought your cases explained. Please, come in.' Shipley held an arm out for them to go into the house.

There was an equestrian centre directly opposite across the road, but Harry couldn't see any horses, scabby or otherwise.

'Your luggage is in your rooms. We had three spare, so two of you will be sharing.'

They looked at each other like four gunslingers waiting for the first one to draw.

'Harry McNeil and Calvin Stewart, you both have your own rooms. Dunbar and Evans, you have to share, I'm afraid.'

'He'll no' be the only one who's afraid if you fucking sleepwalk and end up in my pit. I swear to Christ,' Dunbar said to Evans.

'Vice versa. I don't want you climbing in with me.'

'I don't know what you pair of shaggers are whispering about,' said Stewart, 'but if I get woken up by any funny noises coming from your room tonight, somebody will be getting their baws booted.'

'What kind of funny noises, sir?' Dunbar asked. 'You mean wildlife after we've left our window open?' Dunbar looked at his boss, his own imaginary lighter setting fire to the bigger man.

'If that's what you want to call it.' Stewart thumped up the stairs ahead of the other men.

'That victim won't be the only one losing a fucking finger,' Evans said to Dunbar in a low voice.

'No' fuckin' deef, Evans,' came the shout from the landing above.

Shipley looked at the others as if he hadn't heard right, but the others ignored him.

'Lead the way, squire. You have real fires in here?'

'Oh, no. We converted to gas years ago. There are no fires in here.'

Don't count on it. 'Do you serve dinner?'

'Just bed and breakfast, I'm afraid. My wife used to offer such things, but she isn't as fit as she used to be. They serve meals along the road in the Orr Arms Hotel.'

'Fair enough.'

'Or there's a fish and chip shop, but that's further along,' Shipley said at the landing. They saw Stewart waiting, one hand in his pocket, and they knew the DSup was playing with his lighter again.

Shipley handed them the keys to their rooms. 'First on the left, Stewart. Second, McNeil. The one across the way is the remainder. Your colleague put your luggage away. Breakfast is at seven to nine. Enjoy your stay, gentlemen.'

Shipley turned and walked away while Stewart opened his door. 'That wee specky bastard better no' have been going through my fucking suitcase,' he said, turning to the others. 'Did you lot bring your own pillowcases?'

None of them had.

'Shame on you. Don't come whining to me when your fucking pus is covered in bedbug bites. I'll be turning that mattress upside down, inspecting it. If there's the remotest sign of some creepy-crawly in my bed, that old bawbag will be fucking hearing about it. Just before I burn his fucking mattress oot the back.'

'Right then, I'm going to give Alex a quick call, then we can head out to dinner if you like,' Harry said.

'Sounds like a plan,' Dunbar said. Then to Evans: 'Remember what I said.'

Evans made a face and went into their room.

Harry went into his and was glad to see it was en-suite; he assumed the others were too. He took his iPad out and started a FaceTime call with Alex, remembering he had to call his brother.

'Hi, honey,' Alex said, holding the baby on her lap. 'Grace says hi too, but she's going to have dinner in a minute, so she's catching up on some sleep.'

'How's she been?'

'Terrific. The girls are coming round later, but it's not like the old days where it involved alcohol. I said the others could have a drink if they wanted, but they said no, if I wasn't having any, they wouldn't either.'

'Your sister and Briony are good people.'

'How's Derek?' Alex asked.

'I'll call him after this. He said he was going to go and visit Auntie Ella. I hope he found out where she lives. I haven't a clue.'

'I wouldn't know where anything is in Inverness anymore either.'

There was silence for a moment. 'What do you mean, *anymore*?'

'I told you that we used to live in Inverness when I

was little. My dad came from Inverness and we would go and visit my aunt and uncle after we left, just like Derek's doing.'

'You never told me that.'

'I did, Harry. A long time ago. You just don't listen.' She laughed and smiled at the baby. 'Your daddy doesn't listen, does he? No, he doesn't.'

'Aw, that's nice; teach the bairn things about her dad that aren't true. She'll grow up thinking I'm daft in the heid.'

Alex looked at him. 'Don't worry; she knows I'm just kidding. Anyway, how's your room?'

Harry wondered how Alex knew that Grace knew she was just kidding. Maybe these things were subliminal, like when you played classical music to your child when it was still in the woman's womb.

'We're in the town where the murder happened. Muir of Ord. We thought we'd be staying in Inverness itself, but somebody somewhere must have thought this was a good idea. Still, the guest house is fine. I feel knackered, to be honest. It's been a long day. A lot of running about.'

'I still miss it. I'm going to be glad to get back to work.'

'That's the same attitude that a jilted lover might have after being asked if they want to start the relationship up again. It seems like a good idea, then things go back to the way they were.'

'Harry, you need to brush up on your pep talk skills.' She laughed, then the doorbell rang.

'That will be your sister. She's going to help put Grace down, then hopefully Briony will be here soon. Talk to you tomorrow, lover boy.'

'Night, honey. Love you both.'

He waited for Alex to cut the connection before dialling his brother's number on his phone, folding the iPad down.

'Derek, it's me. Where are you? We got billeted in Muir of Ord, just outside of Inverness. Give me a call when you get this.'

He had a quick shower before meeting the others downstairs in the lounge.

'I'm fucking starvin',' Stewart said, and a man stood up, diverting his attention from the TV.

'You arr ee peeg,' he said to Stewart. A woman, presumably his wife, was sitting looking, putting out a hand for her husband to sit down.

'François, don't bother.' She was obviously Scottish, married to this European.

'What did you say?' Stewart said, standing up. He dwarfed the man, who didn't bat an eye.

'You heard me, you eegnorant swine. Apologise to my waf.'

'The fuck you think you're talking to, ya wee shite? I'll knock you fuckin' out.'

'I weel take you outside,' the man started to say, poking Stewart in the chest. He didn't get a chance to say any more. Stewart grabbed his finger and bent it, causing the man to get down on his knees. The woman squealed and jumped up.

'Do that once more, fuck face, and I will arrest you for assaulting a police officer.' Stewart brought his handcuffs round and dangled them in front of the man's face. The tourist looked at Dunbar and Harry for help, but Dunbar just nodded.

'Okay, okay, I not mean to harm you. Sorree.'

Stewart let him go and smiled at Dunbar. 'Come on, Evans can drive us and stay sober. He's still buying, mind.' He put his handcuffs away.

'That's fine, sir, I don't mind,' Evans said, and Stewart smiled and marched out. Evans whispered to Dunbar, 'Then I'll pass the tab to accounts under miscellaneous. I'm fucked if I'm going to get reamed with his bar bill.'

'Bawbag! Fuckin' hurry up!'

'Go to Inverness, they said. It'll be fun, they said,' Dunbar uttered as they left the guest house.

'Your car or ours, Harry?' Evans said.

'You're a comedian, son,' Harry said, standing by the Glasgow pool car.

'I thought you might say that.' They piled in like a bunch of teenage joyriders and the drive down to the Orr Arms Hotel took thirty seconds.

There was a minibus parked outside with the name of some obscure backpacking tour company name on the side.

'This is a lively wee place for being out in the wilds,' Stewart said, and they managed to find a table in the bar. Evans went up for the drinks and told the barman they would be wanting dinner. When they were settled with their drinks, a young woman came over with her notepad.

'Evening, gentlemen. May I take your order?'

Stewart managed to order his food and not utter a swear word until she had gone. There was a buzz in the bar.

'I wish my local was like this. Where I drink, some bastard would have been stabbed by now.'

'Tell us how you know Jill Craig, Calvin,' Dunbar said.

'We used to be stationed together. She was a real go-getter. I'm not surprised she's in charge. Got a real good heid on her shoulders.'

'Any history there?' Harry asked.

Stewart sipped his pint, some foam sitting on his upper lip before he wiped it away. 'I wish. You might not have noticed, but she's a lot younger than me. I know I had table manners once upon a long time ago, but she was on the fast track. She was in Helen Street for a while, before Jimmy transferred there. She was DCI back then. But that was just a stepping stone for her.'

'She moved to Inverness for her promotion?' Harry asked.

'Aye. She came from here originally. She made DSup and came back home.'

'She'll know all about the Nightmare Man then?' Dunbar said.

'She does. She was in her twenties when the killings happened. She was just about to start training at Tulliallan. It was a scary time, she said.'

'And now it's landed in her lap,' Evans said.

'Aye. She's more than capable of handling it, though.'

Their food came, served by the smiling girl and another young man. It looked good and smelled good, and as they tucked in, tasted just as good.

'I wonder if they have any spare rooms,' Stewart said. 'Instead of being lumped in with that twat along the road.'

'I doubt it. This will be the first place people will want to stay at.'

'Aye. Somebody dropped the ball there,' Dunbar said.

'At least we can get scran here,' Stewart said. 'What about Liz Aitken? She said she was going to take us to a few bars.'

'I hardly think she said that,' Harry said. 'She's going to have a couple of drinks with us.'

'You'd better watch yourself, Harry. Liz is a fine-looking young woman and she's got an eye for you,' Stewart said with a grin.

'What? Away with yourself. I'm married with a wee yin.'

'Aye, Jimmy was telling me you had a wee yin, right enough.'

Dunbar laughed. 'Calvin talking pish and he's only had a sip of lager. You should see him when we have to chuck him into a fast black.'

'The last time you pair of bastards put me in a taxi, my wallet was empty when I woke up next morning.'

'It was bloody empty when we put you in it,' Dunbar said. 'Robbie and I had to club together with a big tip just so the driver would take you home.'

'That's what friends are for.'

Dunbar gave Harry a quick look, trying to tell him that he wasn't friends with Stewart, it was just a figure of speech.

Then Harry's phone rang. He took it out and looked at the screen. 'Sorry, lads, I have to take this.'

'Nae bother, son,' Stewart said.

Harry stood up and took the phone out into the reception area. 'Derek. Where are you just now?'

'I was with Auntie Ella this afternoon. Jesus, she's looking old now, Frank.'

'She *is* old, Derek.'

'Aye, I know that, but she looks *old. You know what I'm saying. But we chatted for a while. Caught up with old times.'*

'Where are you now?' Harry repeated.

'I'm at a bar in the city centre. Where are your digs?'

'In Muir of Orr, the wee town where Hannah Keddie was found murdered. Is Auntie Ella okay with you staying at her place?'

'I was going to ask her, but she seemed so frail. I just found a nice hotel in the city centre.'

'You going to meet us for a pint later on?'

'Love to, brother, but I bumped into an old friend of mine.'

'Aw fuck off, Derek. I've heard that line before. Is it some blonde who just happens to be a barmaid now?'

'Deary me. If I was thin-skinned, I might take offence at that.'

'I just know you, brother.'

'You don't have to worry, Harry. My friend is indeed a female. But that's all it is.'

'So you're not meeting us later?'

'I'll be around for a few days, Harry. If your case

goes on longer, I can still run the business from here. I have my laptop and I just need to keep in touch with the tenants in the rental properties we have.'

'What's the name of this hotel?'

'The Mercure. Overlooking the Ness. I'll catch up with you tomorrow, Harry. Got to go. Stay safe.'

Derek disconnected the call and Harry walked back into the bar.

'Bad news?' Dunbar asked.

'Just my brother being an arse. He's met an old friend of his, he says.'

'And you don't believe him?' Stewart said.

'No, not for one minute. I know what he's like.'

'Is somebody going to call Liz Aitken?' Evans asked.

'You can give her a call, son,' Stewart said. 'Ask her where we can meet her.'

'I'll finish this first.'

SIXTEEN

'Thanks for meeting me here, Derek,' DCS Jill Craig said.

'It's been a long time, Jill. All my fault, of course. I should have called you.'

Jill smiled at him and put a hand on his. 'It's fine.'

'You've done well for yourself.'

'So have you.'

'Eventually,' Derek said, standing up. 'Refill?'

'Thanks.'

He picked up her empty glass and headed to the bar. He got a tonic for her and another glass of Coke for himself and headed back to their table, which was a semi-circular booth in the far corner. They were in the Mercure bar, amid other guests and visitors.

'Hardly a jumping nightclub,' Derek said, sitting back down.

'We're hardly the age for that anymore,' she said, sipping her drink.

He laughed. 'I'm worried about falling and needing a hip replacement. Cheers.'

'Do you think Harry is going to be angry when he finds out who you were drinking with?'

'Probably. He'll have a million questions, but I was able to cadge a lift from him to get up here, and he went for it. It was much better than me coming here and him suddenly bumping into me. Your idea to go through and talk to him in person was good advice.'

'It's just using a bit of psychology.'

'If he only knew why we were really here.'

'It's got to be between us right now, Derek,' Jill said.

'I know.' He sipped the Coke, wishing it was a pint of lager, but he knew he had to stay sober.

They talked about old times, about growing up in Inverness, how they both moved away and followed different paths.

Harry called again. They couldn't get hold of their friend so they were just going to stay in the wee hotel they were in with a view to having a few sociable beers and an early night.

'They're going to get pished,' Derek said.

Jill laughed. 'You still have a way with words.'

'You know me, Jill; I like to say it like it is.'

'Come on then, let's get going.'

'What kind of car do you drive?' he asked her as they made their way out of the back door.

'Lamborghini.'

'You jest.'

'Of course I jest. I drive a police issue Vauxhall. It was either that or use my own car and I didn't have my own car.'

'Police issue it is then.'

They walked into the car park, which overlooked the River Ness. It looked spectacular in the gloaming with the lights coming on. Not quite full dark but well on its way. Jill stood next to him and spoke without looking at him.

'You ready for this?'

'Not really. How can I be?' Derek looked at her, studied the outline of her face – the strong jaw, the bright eyes, the perfectly shaped nose.

After some moments of silence, she turned to him. 'You're sure Harry doesn't have any idea?'

'I'm sure.'

'We should tell him. I've said that from the beginning.'

'We can't, Jill. We can't know for sure, so we can't tell him. Not until the proper time.'

'I hope we're wrong.' Jill looked back at the twinkling lights across the river.

'You and me both.'

Jill took a deep breath and let it out slowly, shivering in the cooling evening air.

'Come on, let's go,' she said, opening the doors of her car remotely.

They got in and headed out of Inverness.

SEVENTEEN

'You can always have a few and still drive. It's only up the road,' Stewart said.

'I wouldn't recommend that, son,' a stranger said. 'The polis round here can be bastards. I should know; I'm one of them.'

Stewart stood up, looking down at the man. He reached into his jacket and the policeman stepped forward. 'I've taken down bigger men than you, pal.'

'I'm going to reach into my pocket and I'm going to bring out a wee wallet. When I open said wallet, you, my friend, are royally fucked.' Stewart brought out his warrant card, and by the time Sergeant Bobby McGuire looked at the other men, they were all holding their warrant cards open.

'Oh. I see. Well, I was just giving you some friendly advice, sir.'

'What's your name, son?'

'Sergeant McGuire, sir.'

'McGuire? Sit down and we'll get you another pint. Go on. I would rather bend your ear than break your fucking jaw anyway.' Stewart looked at Evans. 'Go on then, don't keep the man waiting.' He introduced them all.

Some of the others in the pub were looking at Stewart. Harry guessed that it might have been a long time since a fight had taken place in here and a stranger had been on the receiving end, but the locals saw there were four of them and quickly calculated the risk of sticking one on a copper.

McGuire pulled a chair over and Evans went to the bar.

'You found the lassie up in the graveyard, didn't you?' Dunbar asked.

'Aye, that I did. Old Tam drove me up the hill. We have two patrol cars and they were both out, but Glasgow was on the phone and it was urgent, so I asked one of the locals to take me.' McGuire left out the bit about throwing *that bastard bike* over the wall.

'Did you think you were going to find anything?' Harry asked.

'You know the old saying, hope for the best, prepare for the worst. I was hoping to God she wasn't in the graveyard where the lassie was found thirty years ago. I was given a wee bit o' background, like she was some video journalist, and maybe she had fallen and hurt herself. Something like that. So I went up to investigate, and that's when we found her.'

'We?' Stewart said. 'You took the old codger in with you?'

'No' exactly; he followed me in. I had left him sitting in the car. We found her together. One shoe was off, lying at the other mausoleum. Then further along, we found her. Lying in the overgrown grass, all cut up. It was bloody awful.'

Evans came back with the pint. 'Cheers.'

'Were you around here when the first murders took place?' Harry asked.

'We lived in Inverness back then. I was fifteen at the time. I'd heard the stories of the Nightmare Man of course, but I thought it was all a load of shite. We used to take our girlfriends into a graveyard and scare them a bit for a laugh. It was all fun, then the first girl was murdered. Bloody well scared the shite out of all of us. We started to hang out at each other's houses after that. Nobody thought it was some nutter from here; everybody thought it was somebody living in Inverness.'

'Do you remember any names bandied about at the time?' Dunbar asked. 'Any rumours?'

'Are you kidding me? The rumour mill was in top flight. Every man and his dog was suspected. You couldn't go out for a loaf of bread on your own but people thought you were away out killing somebody. Fear gripped everybody, including my folks. And my dad was a police officer just like us.'

'What was his name?' Harry asked, maybe a little too quickly, he thought, then sipped his pint, hiding behind the glass.

'Billy McGuire. He was based in Inverness.'

'Is he still around?' Dunbar asked.

'Naw. He died of his injuries after getting knocked down by a car. They never got the bastard. He was in a coma for a month before they pulled the plug. He was the only family I had left, except for my own family, like. I didn't want them living in Inverness. I preferred to be out here; that's why I put in for a transfer.'

'But one of the girls was originally found here,' Evans said, not following the man's logic. Why would he want to bring his family to one of the locations where a victim was found?

'As I said, they figured the killer was living in Inverness. They never got him. A lot of folks didn't believe he ever left. I did. I mean, killers like that will keep on killing unless they're stopped.'

'Unless they have an agenda,' Stewart said, finishing his pint.

'True. But when they looked at all those girls, they didn't have anything in common. They were just random victims.'

'You remember Colin Harris from up here?' Dunbar asked. He kept his voice low so the other regulars wouldn't hear him.

'Aye, I remember my old man talking about him. He tried to kill a copper who had cornered him, but the copper ended up killing him in self-defence. What was that copper's name again?'

'Willie Dowd,' Harry said, putting his glass back down. 'Harris was working down in Edinburgh, and probably Glasgow too, but he fled north back home. Some detectives from down there came here looking for him. That's when he attacked Willie Dowd and paid for it with his life. Colin Harris was the Tattoo Artist.'

He didn't explain about Willie Dowd's son-in-law, Jeremy Wilson, being a killer too. They had figured that Harris was manipulated by Wilson, but Harry didn't want to go into a long, drawn-out explanation here.

'Aye. Willie Dowd. I wonder what happened to him? Him and his cronies. Robert Briggs for one. My dad told me all about him. He was a bit of a bastard. He put in for a transfer after a while. My dad said Briggs felt slighted. He was in charge of the Nightmare Man case and some bigwig walked in and took over.'

'Willie Dowd died of a heart attack. He had dementia,' Harry said.

'Sorry to hear that. My dad knew him and said he was a good bloke. But he and some others transferred out after that case. It hit a lot of coppers really hard, including my old man. I can't blame the others for leaving. I can't remember the other bloke's name. There was Briggs, Dowd and somebody else. All three of them thought highly of my dad.'

Dunbar looked at Harry and gave his head a very subtle shake. Nobody wanted to explain about Harry's dad being the third amigo when McGuire Senior worked here. They didn't know the present McGuire well enough to feel comfortable talking about Harry's now-deceased father.

'Did you know that Colin Harris is buried here?' McGuire said.

'We did,' Stewart answered. 'The press were given some shitey story about him being cremated and his ashes scattered, to stop the ghouls from going to his grave.'

'Aye, some people know, but not enough people care now. It wasn't widely publicised, but my dad knew. I was just starting out on the force, so I knew through my dad, but a lot of the others weren't told.

He's buried in a corner of the graveyard with a little marker. The one where I found that lassie.'

'The other two victims were killed shortly afterwards, weren't they?' Harry said.

'They were. Sophie Allander and Josie Brown. Before their murders, there were rumours of a man wearing black creeping about. My dad and some of his colleagues checked it out, but they thought it was just some lassies' imaginations running wild. The Nightmare Man. The old myth. Then Karen McPherson was murdered. That took it to a whole new level. The others swore they saw a man in black in the woods, but it never panned out. They were seventeen, into drinking and smoking, and the graveyard was a favourite haunt for the teenagers to hang out where they could drink without getting caught. That's where they found Sophie and Josie. They knew where to look. They were murdered in the same spot as Karen, more or less. Near the mausoleum. It was the night of the candlelight vigil for Karen.'

'Jesus,' Dunbar said. 'And to this day, they still don't know if they did see somebody creeping about.'

'Correct. And after that, the killings stopped. There was speculation of course: did the killer die? Was he sent to prison? Did he move and start killing somewhere else? There were never any reports of women being murdered and having *I am Nightmare* carved into their chests. Not that we ever found out.'

Harry sat with an uneasy feeling. One he hadn't had since he'd sold his dad's car.

The one with the amputated finger in it.

EIGHTEEN

Jill Craig sat with the lights out. The police tape that had been strung across the entrance to the old grave-yard fluttered in the breeze. Nobody was here anymore. Normally forensics would be at a scene for more than a day, but there was nothing here to exam-ine. Long grass, weeds and blood spatter on the side of a mausoleum. They had spent more than a day combing the place for a discarded cigarette or some kind. of wrapper, and had found nothing. No empty beer cans from drunk teenagers. No discarded condoms.

Jill put the car in gear again and slowly drove round the track and stopped at the archway.

'Are you going to drive through it?' Derek asked.

She turned off the engine and looked at him. 'I

want to walk from here. If he walked with Hannah
Keddie, or ran after her, I want to see what she saw.'

They got out of the car and walked through the
arch, then turned right and walked beside tall trees that
were waving in the wind. She pulled a small torch out
of her pocket and turned it on. Derek used the light
from his phone.

'Makes it more creepy, swinging a light about,'
Derek said.

'Don't be scared; Jill's here to look after you.'

He wasn't sure if she was joking or not, but he
laughed anyway.

'Do you miss your ex-husband?' Derek asked,
trying not to jump when a sudden gust of wind
whipped through the graveyard. They turned left,
walking along towards the mausoleums.

Jill started running, taking off at a fair clip.

Derek's heart thumped up into his mouth and he
took off after her, but as soon as they came level with
the mausoleums, she stopped and turned round.

Derek whipped round too, not sure if flight had
now become fight.

There was nothing there.

'He grabbed her here, and she fought with him.
Her shoe came off, they carried on fighting and he
dragged her round to the side here, where he stabbed
her. Then carved the words after she was dead.'

Derek was dismayed to see he was the only one out of breath.

Jill looked at him. 'What did you see coming in here?'

'Trees. A church. Old gravestones.'

'That's right, and I read the report of the other gravestones being graffitied. They were in well-kept cemeteries. I had forensics walk this whole graveyard, looking at every single gravestone. Not one has graffiti on it. This guy Eric Straw lured her here. She trusted him, but something went awry and she ran – through that archway and into here. He caught up with her and he killed her.'

'Why would he kill her?' Derek asked. 'What was his motive?'

'I don't know yet. Come on. Let's go further along. Let's go and see Colin Harris.'

'I know the Harris family was big around here. I think that mausoleum belongs to the family, erected by Colin's great-grandfather. I can see why they didn't want him in there beside them. Black sheep of the family.'

They walked to the end of the graveyard and the grass and weeds were completely out of control here, worse than at the mausoleums.

'Do you know where it is?' Derek asked.

'Over here, just down from the corner a bit. I've

been here before.'

They shone their lights around at the ivy-covered wall, at the trees hanging over them from both sides of the wall. They knew that on the other side were woods. It couldn't have been a nice, new housing development, Derek thought. No, it was woods, which were a million times more creepy than this place and that was saying something.

'Look at that,' Jill said, shining her torch at something beige. She reached over and picked it up. It was a doll who'd had her hands tied with thread. A red line, now faded, had been drawn across her throat. One finger was missing from her right hand and her feet were missing.

'Holy Christ. What the hell is that?' Derek said.

'Some twisted person left this here for visitors. Reminding anybody who is foolish enough to come here just what Colin was.' She threw the doll back down and looked at the inscription on the headstone: Just his first name, and underneath just the year of his birth and the year of his death.

Derek looked around him in the dark. The small lights were distorting his night vision and he kept thinking he could see something creeping about.

'You know, what we're about to do doesn't really prove anything.'

'We have to try. If we do find something then...'

She shrugged. 'It will prove your dad was telling the truth.'

'Or it will prove that he was guilty all along.'

'Let's not jump to conclusions.'

They walked back to the car, Derek proud of himself that he didn't squeal once. He felt a sense of relief wash over him when they got back into the car and his heart rate started to slow back down to normal when Jill's car started first time. He almost jumped up and down when they left the graveyard and headed back down to town.

When Jill parked up outside the house, Derek looked out of his window at the light behind the curtains. 'She's still up. I was worried that she was an early-to-bed, early-to-rise person.'

'Let's go and give her a knock before she decides to get upstairs with a good book.'

'I'll text her that I'm outside and would like her to meet you.'

Jill looked surprised. 'Text?'

'Yes. She has a phone in case of emergencies.'

'Smart lady. Go ahead, Derek, give her a wee text.'

Derek took his phone out and fired off a text to the number the old woman had given him that afternoon. It was answered almost right away.

'She said to come in. She's looking forward to

meeting you. But please remember the story we concocted.'

'I remember it. I think I have enough straight in my head to pull it off.'

'If not, then...well, I don't have a Plan B.'

They got out of the car and walked up to the door. The woman had been waiting behind it and she swung it open.

'Derek! Back again! So nice of you to bring your girlfriend round. Come away in.' She stepped back and the couple walked in, and Derek led Jill through to the living room.

'Girlfriend?' Jill said.

'Just roll with it.'

The old woman came into the room.

'Auntie Ella, this is Jill Craig, my girlfriend. Jill, this is Auntie Ella.'

The women shook hands. 'Good to meet you. Has Derek been telling you all about me?'

'Only nice things.'

'Sit down and I'll go and put the kettle on.'

They sat down next to each other on the couch and they heard the old woman bustling about in the kitchen, putting the kettle on and clacking about with cups.

'Derek!' the old woman then shouted. 'Come and give me a hand with the cups, sweetheart.'

'So you *are* domesticated?' Jill said, laughing, as Derek got up off the couch.

'You should see me open a can of soup. I'm a dab hand in the kitchen.'

'I believe it.' She laughed as he left the living room and listened to them clattering about with stuff. Then a few minutes later, Derek walked in with a tray and laid it down on the dining table.

Ella followed and sat down in her chair while Derek poured from the teapot, already wearing its comfy pyjamas in the form of a tea cosy.

'What do you take in yours?' Jill asked the old woman.

'Just milk. I try cutting back on sugar. I know we're all going to end up in a box one day, but it's how fast you're going to get there that counts.'

'Very true.' Jill poured milk into the tea and handed the cup over.

'You don't look like you have to worry about your figure, dear. What is it you do for a living again?'

'I work in an office.'

'I worked in a supermarket when I was younger. My husband, Derek's Uncle Kit, worked in a furniture store. He was a manager. We did very well, but we lived frugally.'

Derek sat down and put his cup in front of him on the table. Jill sipped her tea.

'Listen, Auntie Ella, I was wondering if you still had that box of toys here. The one Harry and I played with when we came round. You said you were going to keep them here when we came back for a visit.'

'It's still up in the attic.'

'Would you mind if I go up and bring it down? I'm sure Harry would be pleased to see the toys too.'

'Hold on one second,' Ella said, putting her cup down.

She got up and left the room and they heard her go into the kitchen.

'Did that sound convincing?' Derek whispered.

'You were that good, you should be on the stage,' Jill replied.

They were both quiet when they heard Ella switch the light off and come back into the living room. She was holding out a carrier bag wrapped round something. It was frozen.

'Is this what you've really come for?' Ella asked. She unrolled the bag and little pieces of ice fell off onto the carpet.

Derek and Jill sat staring at the old woman.

'I found it in the attic when I was putting the toy box away,' Ella said, handing over the now-open bag.

Derek looked in before putting a hand in and bringing the object out.

It was a finger.

It had pink nail polish, faded but still discernible.

Jill looked at it. 'I just read the file. The first victim from thirty years ago, Karen McPherson, was wearing pink nail polish.'

'Work in an office? I know you're a detective, Jill. And you're looking for Hannah Keddie's killer. But back then, three lassies were murdered. And I think I know who did it: Derek and Harry's father. George McNeil, my brother, was a serial killer.'

NINETEEN

Harry was expecting Stewart to be singing 'Flower of Scotland', staggering around, but the big bastard could hold his drink.

'Where's the fucking chippie round here?' he asked.

'God Almighty, Calvin,' Dunbar replied, 'you've just had your dinner.'

'I'm only asking for future reference. That was a smashing meal in there. Great wee place. If only all wee hotels were as good as that. Not like fucking Harvey Shipman's place.'

'Shipley. You're mixing him up with the serial killer Shipman.'

'I know what I'm saying, son. I've only had a few beers. I'm not exactly rolling about on the ground pished, puking behind cars and having a piss in the bushes. Just drive us.'

They piled in the car, Evans promising that he would arse the half-bottle he'd brought with him. Harry was surprised that none of them were falling about, but after they'd got talking to McGuire, all they had was a couple of pints.

'I'm getting fucking old,' Stewart said. 'Out on a Saturday night and going home sober. That's all your fault, Jimmy.'

'Me? How's that?'

'You should have insisted that we get pished.'

'You're here for a wee rest, remember?'

Evans drove them the thirty seconds back to the guest house. Norman Bates was waiting for them at the front door.

The older man stepped forward. 'I hope you're happy,' he said to Stewart.

'I'm always happy, cock. Thanks for asking.'

'I mean, I hope you're happy that the Martins are gone.'

'If I knew who the Martins were, maybe I would consider it.'

'They're the French couple you assaulted,' Shipley said.

'Is that what he's calling it? He assaulted a police

officer. No wonder he's legged it. I was going to have this place overrun with officers first thing tomorrow morning. With a search warrant. He looked well dodgy, and they don't like it upstairs when one of their own has to defend himself from attack. And in front of witnesses too. Imagine the headlines when the reporters come knocking, son: "B&B owner harbours dangerous fugitive from the law". Because that's what he is now, a fugitive.'

'What? No, that can't be. My reputation would be ruined.'

'I can make this go away, son. Like it never even happened.'

'How can you do that?'

'Just get the missus to put clean sheets on the bed in the room the Martins were staying in, and DCI Dunbar will move into it tonight. And we'll make sure you get the going rate, of course, so you won't lose money.'

'You would do that?'

Stewart put his arm around the man's shoulders. 'Aye. For you I would. Just make sure you have some extra tattie scones for breakfast in the morning.'

Shipley beamed a smile. 'I'll get the sheets and make sure the potato scones are defrosted. Thank you, Calvin.'

'Go at it, Harvey.'

He let the man go and he scarpered away into the guest house.

Dunbar shook his head. 'I've never heard such drivel in my life.'

Stewart smiled. 'I do have a way with words, don't I?'

'That's one way of putting it,' Evans said.

'Takes years of practice, son.'

They walked into the guest house and the little bar in the living room was lit up. Shipley was behind it. 'Can I offer you gentlemen a pint? On the house.'

'You didn't say this place had a bar,' Stewart said to Dunbar.

'Who knew?'

It was clearly open to the public but catered for older guests, judging by the music. A TV was playing on a shelf in one corner, muted. Two couples sat at tables, and they could only be guests. Stewart couldn't see anybody from the small town making this place their local.

'Aye, that would be smashing,' Stewart said, and the general consensus was that it would indeed be acceptable. Professional Standards might look on it differently, but Harry wasn't in that department anymore and his thirst overcame his sense of duty.

Then his phone rang as Shipley poured the pints.

'*Harry, it's me. Can I meet you somewhere?*' Derek said.

'Of course. Do you want to come over here to the hotel?'

'*I think Jimmy Dunbar should hear this. Just him and you. Can you make that happen? I don't want the older bloke there, or the younger one.*'

'You can come up to my room. Or I can come along to your hotel if you like.'

'*It would be better at your hotel. We're in Muir of Orr just now.*'

'We?'

'*I'll explain shortly, Harry. I just need to talk to you and Dunbar.*'

'Come along then. Wait in your car and I'll text you when you can come in. We're having a beer in the hotel's bar just now. It's a quiet place. We shouldn't be long. I'll give Jimmy a heads-up.'

They had a pint and Harry was relieved when Stewart announced it was past his bedtime. Sarcasm at its finest. 'I'll see you lot of shaggers at breakfast.'

Shipley's wife made an appearance in the doorway. 'That's the room ready now,' she said with a smile.

'Go on then, heid,' said Dunbar to Evans, 'you can take it. I can't be arsed moving all my stuff. And don't be all night. I'll be coming up in a wee while to speak to Cathy on FaceTime.'

'Give Scooby a kiss from me.'

'I'll give you a fucking kick from him more like.'

Evans laughed and he and Stewart left the small bar.

'Jimmy, I need to have a word.'

'What's up, Harry? You look like you've seen a ghost.'

'Derek asked if he and a friend of his could have a word. In private.'

'Sounds a bit mysterious.'

'You're telling me. He's been acting weird. Then he calls me and tells me he met up with an old friend. And now I think he's bringing her here. I hope to Christ it's not to tell me he's leaving Briony for her and moving up here permanently.'

'Let's hear what he has to say. Residents' lounge?'

'As long as nobody else is in there.'

Dunbar looked at Shipley. 'Any chance we could use your lounge for a little meeting? We have a couple of friends coming in.'

'Oh, sure, that's okay. Take as long as you need.'

Harry wondered if the man had anything to hide and would now do anything to appease Stewart.

'Good man.' Dunbar looked at Harry. 'Give him a call.'

Harry took his phone out and fired off a text to his

brother. A few minutes later, Derek walked in. With Jill Craig.

'Evening, ma'am,' Harry said.

'Let's just use Jill for now. Lead us to the lounge.'

Dunbar walked ahead and showed Jill into the room, assuring her that they wouldn't be disturbed.

'This better be good,' Harry said to Derek.

TWENTY

The four of them sat in the room with the TV off. Harry sat beside Dunbar on one couch while Derek sat with Jill on the other.

'You didn't recognise me, Harry, did you?' Jill said. 'When we met at the station earlier.'

'Well, I was thinking you looked a little bit familiar, but...no. No, I didn't. Sorry.'

'Don't be sorry. We grew up together. I moved away to Glasgow not long after you and Derek moved down to Fife. I knew Mel. We used to play together. She might remember me.'

'She does,' Derek confirmed. 'I already mentioned you to her.'

'I'm assuming you're not here to reminisce,' Harry said.

'No,' Jill replied. 'It's to do with the Nightmare Man, I'm afraid.' She looked directly at Harry.

He thought she had grown into a very beautiful woman and wondered if there was a significant other waiting at home. He didn't see a wedding ring, but that didn't mean anything. He was sure Derek would know the answer.

'Let's start at the beginning,' Derek said, looking at Jill. She smiled at him.

'Okay. I bumped into Derek one day when I was down in Edinburgh. We've kept in touch ever since. We talked about old times and I told him I had been a university graduate fast-tracked in the police. I was in Glasgow for the longest time, and then I moved back up to Inverness so I could take the post of detective chief superintendent. Things have been fine here, but I read about the case with the Tattoo Artist. And how he had died in a fire. I mean, I know Colin Harris got the blame a long time ago, but we only recently discovered he had an accomplice and that man was DI Willie Dowd's son-in-law, Jeremy Wilson.'

The three men sat looking at her, waiting for her to get to the punchline.

'I think Jeremy Wilson might still be alive.'

'Before we go any further, ma'am,' Dunbar said, 'if you don't mind, I'd like to get DS Evans down here. He needs to hear this.'

'I'm not sure that's a good idea,' Jill replied.

'When we were dealing with Wilson, he tried to shoot Harry's son, Chance. Harry's wife, DS Alex Maxwell, jumped in front of her stepson and took the bullet for him. Both DS Evans and I stabilised Alex until the ambulance crew arrived. Young Robbie and I have been through a lot together. I'd trust him with my life.'

Jill sat and thought about this for a moment. 'Okay, call him and get him down here.'

Dunbar took his phone out and sent Evans a text: *Heid. Get doon here to the lounge. Right now.*

He sent it and they waited, and a few minutes later, the door was thrown open. 'Right, ya bastard –' Evans started to say but stopped when he saw Jill Craig. 'Apologies, ma'am, but I thought the DCI here was in trouble.' He threw Dunbar a look that suggested that might still be the case when the others left.

'Come in, Robbie and sit down, son,' Dunbar said.

'You're no' dyin, sir?' Evans said.

'Shut your cake hole and listen to what the boss has to say. It's about Jeremy Wilson. She thinks he might still be alive.'

Evans sat down, looked at the faces and waited for a punchline that wasn't coming. 'You can't be serious. We all saw him go down and that basement room was well alight. He didn't come back out. They pulled a body from the rubble. We all signed a sworn affidavit saying it was Wilson in there.'

'We all thought he was in there, Robbie,' Jill said. 'I more than anybody. Until I got this.' She took a slip of paper out of her handbag and opened it up for Harry and Dunbar to read.

Hello Jill. I thought you might like to know I'm back. And just to show you that I want you to play the game again, I'm going to start the ball rolling.

'That was put through my letterbox sometime Thursday night. Late. It wasn't there when I went to check the door was locked at around eleven thirty. It was on the doormat at seven,' Jill said.

Dunbar let Evans have a read of it, then he passed it back to Jill.

'That's a copy. I wrote it word for word. The original is in the lab getting tested. I wasn't going to take it seriously until we found Hannah Keddie dead.' She looked at Harry. 'Was DNA testing done to confirm identity?'

'No. As Robbie said, we all signed sworn affidavits confirming that we had seen Jeremy Wilson in the fire and that he was incapacitated. When they eventually dug him out of the rubble, there was nothing left of him. Burnt to a crisp and every bone in his body broken. He was a shell when they brought him out.'

'His wife, Lisa, will be devastated,' Evans said. 'I

spoke to her weeks later and she was finding it hard, knowing her little boy's father was a serial killer.'

'I haven't been able to find her,' Jill says. 'I didn't meet her, but I was going to introduce myself to her and ask her subtle questions. Nobody's seen her in a long time, and we think she's using an alias now. I don't blame her, but she and her little boy may be in danger.'

'He showed no signs of harming them before,' Harry said.

'Who knows what he might do now, though?' Derek said. 'If he's unbalanced, he might do anything.'

'Did you recognise Jeremy Wilson?' Evans asked.

'Not really. After I got the note, I started becoming even more aware of my surroundings.'

'Why would Wilson target you?' Harry asked.

'He knew my father. We all knew him and his family. He used to live round here. It's where he met Willie Dowd and Dowd's daughter. Wilson was a psychologist up here and he became the Northern Constabulary's psychologist. The therapist people would go to after a particularly bad road accident or the like. Somebody they could talk to.'

'Was he a good friend of your father's?'

'He was. They stayed in touch over the years, all of them. Your dad. Willie Dowd. My father even went as far as starting to write books with Wilson.'

Harry was stunned into silence for a moment.

'Your father was...'

'Robert Briggs.'

'I didn't realise,' he said after a few moments. Robert Briggs. Harry pictured the man sitting in the woodworking basement under Willie Dowd's house, a bullet in his head. Jeremy Wilson had killed him, and he had intended to kill Harry, Alex and Chance, and frame Briggs for the murder-suicide.

'You didn't have much to do with your dad, over the years?'

Jill shook her head. 'We had a falling-out. He told me to get out of his life and I thought he was just angry, but he wouldn't return my calls or my letters. I moved on with my life. I got married, but he didn't come to the wedding. He cut me out of his life entirely.'

'He was protecting you, Jill,' Harry said.

'What do you mean?'

'Your sister, Anna, had her finger and feet cut off. It was made to look like an accident, but it was Colin Harris who did that. Under orders from Wilson. It was a way to keep your dad quiet. He must have been petrified. Even before he died, he kept quiet about what had happened because of your niece, his granddaughter. Katie is my son's girlfriend. He probably wanted you to keep your distance because if you were close, then you might have been on Wilson's radar.'

Jill looked shocked. 'I thought all this time he was

just being an ignorant old fool. Now you're telling me he was protecting me.'

'That's about the size of it.'

'I find it hard to believe that Wilson is back,' Dunbar said. 'But just to play Devil's advocate, what if he is? Why is he killing now?'

'I only came back to Inverness a few months ago,' said Jill. 'I was in Fife, then Glasgow. Then I took the promotion up here, and to be honest, it felt good to be coming home. Although I have no family here.'

'Somehow, somebody knows you're back here and wants to take up the game again. And what better way to start it than to kill the old superintendent, Archie Baker? Get him out of the way and then start the killings again,' Harry said. 'And it was reported that somebody stole his file with all the info on the original killings. We should talk to his daughter again.'

Then Harry said, 'There's something you all need to hear.'

'Go on then, mucker, you've got the floor,' Dunbar said.

'You know that my dad bought a car from Willie Dowd years ago. It was a Jaguar XJS. I was cleaning it out before I sold it. I couldn't keep the car any longer, especially after Jeremy Wilson took the shine off it. But when I was checking the jack, I found a dismembered finger. I thought it was Anna Briggs's finger.' He nodded to Jill. 'I thought that maybe Wilson had put it there after he cut it off your sister. I threw it away. In the back of my mind, I was protecting my dad. It'll be long buried in a landfill by now.'

'We'll never know who it belonged to,' Jill said.

'Talking of fingers...' Derek brought out a plastic bag, rolled up. He uncurled it and brought out an old finger, wrapped in cling film. Unrecognisable.

'What the hell is that?' Harry asked.

'It's a finger. Much like the one you found in Dad's car, I imagine.'

'Where did you get it?' Dunbar asked.

Derek looked between Harry and Jill before answering. 'I got it from Auntie Ella,' he said. 'She told us that it was hidden up in the attic. She found it by accident years ago and kept it in her freezer, not knowing what to do with it.'

'And she gave it to you? Just like that?' Harry said.

Jill looked at him. 'She did. She heard about Hannah's murder and thought this was all starting up again. The Nightmare murders. So she wanted to give this to Derek to see if it would help us track down the killer.'

Dunbar looked at Harry. 'Where would your dad have got it?'

'It wasn't him who hid it in the house. When I cornered Jeremy Wilson, he said he controlled Robert

Briggs and Willie Dowd by telling them he had hidden items from the crime scenes that would implicate them. If he got arrested, he would tell the police where those items were, and it would be difficult for them to talk their way out of it. He was blackmailing them. He must have put a finger in my aunt's attic and one in Willie's car. He was very manipulative. He threatened to harm Robert's granddaughter and he married Willie's daughter, just so they would keep quiet.'

'If there was a finger in George McNeil's sister's house and one in Willie Dowd's car, then where is the third one that would incriminate Robert?' Evans asked.

'We don't know.'

'You think Jeremy Wilson was the original Nightmare Man?'

'I don't know, Robbie,' Jill replied. 'I personally think he was involved.'

'The retired cop who was killed in his house, Archie Baker – Stewart said that his daughter knew Wilson and some other weirdo he hung about with. She thought the guy was a police officer but couldn't be sure of his name,' Dunbar said.

'It should be easy to find out,' Derek said.

'We're talking thirty years ago,' Jill said to him. 'It might not be as easy as you think.'

'Stewart said Susan Baker thinks that her father was Eric Straw. He made the name up so he could get to talk to Hannah. Then he became a regular on her podcasts and on her website, but he needed to keep his identity a secret,' Dunbar said.

'Then somebody started spraying the gravestones again,' Harry said. 'Which would have revved Archie Baker up. He got Hannah involved and she came up to Inverness. She was well on board with trying to track down the killer. Imagine the scoop that would have been for her website.'

'Instead, they both ended up murdered,' Jill said.

'If the killer knows you're here and onto him, then you might not be safe,' Derek said. 'Maybe we should see if there're a couple of spare rooms here.'

Dunbar looked at Evans. 'I know of at least one.'

They all looked at Evans. 'Aye, Jill can have my room. I'll get my stuff out of it.'

'Thank you, Robbie. But won't the landlord have something to say?'

'Not if he knows what's good for him,' Dunbar answered.

TWENTY-ONE

Alex woke up with the biggest headache she'd had in a while. It was the stress of getting ready for work and dealing with the bairn. And Grace. She laughed at her own joke. Harry would have found it amusing too.

She had enjoyed last night, but alcohol would have made the evening a little bit easier. She missed the drink, she had to admit, but having the baby made up for it.

No, it didn't. Having Grace in her life was the best thing that had ever happened to her, but not drinking for nine months had been tough. Was that what was really bothering her? No, not really. It was talking to Harry on the phone yesterday that bothered her. She had thought she had told him about living in Inverness when she was little. She remembered when they had gone up to the Highlands to work on the case at the hotel, and Harry had gone on about how he had been born in Inverness and how he had lived there until he was twelve.

She had meant to jump in and say, 'Me too!' Although she had only been two when they left, it was still something they had in common. But having that conversation had passed. Like when you were waiting to join in a conversation, but somebody else thought what they were saying was more important than what you had to say. By the time she remembered, it was too late.

She had thought she had brought up Inverness again, but apparently she hadn't. But what could she really say about it? 'I also lived there when I was a toddler, and my little sister was born later on when we moved down to Edinburgh?' It was maybe a conversation for some winter's night when they were sitting on the couch curled up in front of an old film, but that just hadn't presented itself during their relationship.

Harry hadn't sounded happy about it. Or was that just her imagination? He was working a murder case and he was up to his neck in it. He had also been stressed about Grace, hoping she was going to be born healthy.

The baby started crying and a searing pain shot behind Alex's right eye. Maybe it wasn't the right time to tell Harry that she had started getting migraines.

The doctor said she had to take it easy, that it had been stressful going full term with Grace, that it had taken a lot out of her. She needed to relax, to get plenty of rest and take it easy.

Take it easy!

That was...well, easy for him to say.

Maybe it would be better if she just quit her job and became a full-time mother. But was she ready for that? Or was she just trying to convince herself that she was?

She brewed a coffee and waited for the FaceTime call. She hoped Harry wasn't going to be long. She wanted to go across to the park with Grace.

TWENTY-TWO

Back then

The car's headlight beams cut a swathe through the darkness of the graveyard like a scythe. The place had gone to ruin since they stopped using it. Long grass, weeds poking through the driveway. The church running into disrepair.

He smiled in the car. This place was perfect.

Some of the gravel popped out from under the tyres. The archway was coming up. What a fucking place this was. If it hadn't been for illicit meetings then he wouldn't be coming anywhere near it.

His wife was propped up in front of the TV as usual. He'd suggested an early night on many occasions, but all he got was, *I'm tired. I'm not in the mood.*

When was she going to be in the fucking mood? Not anytime soon, that was for sure.

Well, he knew somebody who would be in the mood. One advantage this place had was that in the summer the trees were in full bloom and offered shade during the day and shelter at night. This was the fourth time he'd come here, and every time his new girl hadn't failed to please him.

He was getting excited just thinking about her. Her soft skin, taut and smooth. Her willingness to do things with him that his wife would never do in a million years.

The car went through the archway and then through the canopy of trees as he turned right. Long tendrils of grass reached out and hit the car like skinny fingers of the dead.

His girlfriend didn't like being alone in here for too long, but he had told her he would drop her off as usual. They just couldn't be seen meeting. He couldn't exactly pull into the bus stop and have her jump in. But he could drop her off when it was dark.

She had reluctantly agreed. Her bravado was bolstered by a few chugs out of the whisky bottle in her dad's cabinet.

He turned left, his headlights picking out the white marble of the mausoleums. The final resting places of those rich bastards. But look at them now: nobody cared about their little funeral homes. Not their ancestors, not the locals. They'd had influence in the town many moons ago, but like all men they'd had to leave this earth the same way they came into it: with nothing. Yes, their parents might have been rich, but they themselves had entered life with nothing on their backs.

His thoughts had started to wander, his hatred for them invading brain space where he should be thinking about his girl.

She had spoken of them running away together, somewhere they could make a fresh start. She was eighteen after all; she wasn't a child anymore. He didn't have the heart to tell her that she wasn't mature enough to run a fucking doll's house, never mind a real one. Would she jump out of bed after they'd made love and go clean the bathroom? Or make him a sandwich? No, she wouldn't. He knew he sounded like a pig when he thought like this, and to voice this to her would be the end, but it was true.

His wife would scuttle away and make him a sandwich after they'd had sex. He couldn't call it *making love* anymore, because there was no love there. Sex. That was it. After being together for years, they knew all there was to know about each other. Nothing was a surprise anymore. Like unwrapping the brown paper parcel from Auntie Flo every Christmas and finding yet another fucking knitted jumper.

He'd made the mistake one year of making a face behind her back and his mother's eyes went wide and he knew then that his arse was going to get tanned afterwards, whether it was Christmas Day or not. He had never made that mistake again.

The next Christmas, he had dug deep. *Oh, Auntie Flo, I love it!* he had said, rushing away through to the bedroom to put it on. It was always some ridiculous pattern that gave ugly Christmas sweaters everywhere a bad name.

His mother had smiled and he had heard her explaining when she thought he was out of earshot that last Christmas he'd had a touch of the flu. Now he was back to normal.

He had come back into the room and the bastard thing made the skin on his arms crawl and his neck itch. And he had to sit with the fucking thing making his skin crawl while the old fuck put a party hat on and drank tea like she had a steel boiler for a bladder.

They all knew when the old cunt got up, it was time for her to have a long piss before heading back home. He waited until she was back in her car, the little European heap of shite that had a funny name, and she honked the horn and waved like she hadn't seen them in years. And then he went to his room and practically ripped the thing off and threw it on the bed. Not even washing it would take the itch out. The only thing he was grateful for was that she didn't want to knit him underpants.

And now his sex life with his wife was like wearing a scabby old itchy sweater. Something that looked like fun to begin with, but you couldn't wait for it to be over.

He had mentally tossed his sex life onto the bed, not wanting to wear it ever again.

He wasn't sure about divorce, though. That might cost him a lot of money. He'd pondered over this for the longest time. Start afresh with a wee lassie who looked like she barely knew how to tie her own shoelaces, or just settle down with the boring wife?

It was hard. This young girl excited him. She told him that he was the best lover she had ever had, but when pressed, admitted he was only the second. She was good-looking, energetic, enthusiastic and willing.

Christ, he was unable to think straight. He'd met her quite a few times, and in his head, he promised himself that each time was going to be the last; then he would tell himself that he would quit after just one more time, like he was trying to kick cigarettes.

He parked the car, keeping the lights on and the engine running. He wasn't stupid. What if the thing broke down? That would call for an explanation he couldn't even begin to think of.

He looked out of the passenger-side window and

couldn't see her. Usually she was waiting at the side of the mausoleum.

Then there was a sudden rapping on the driver's window.

'Boo!' she shouted, smiling and laughing.

He put a hand over his mouth. 'Stupid fucking cow,' he said into the palm of his hand, then he pulled on the door handle, stepping out.

'Did I give you a fright?' Karen McPherson said.

'No, of course not,' he replied, smiling. Inside, his heart was racing, but if his smile slipped now, he wouldn't get what he had come here for and it would all be a waste of time.

She put her arms around his neck and leaned in for a kiss. As her tongue worked its magic, he felt the tension slip away and his hands started roving.

Then she pulled away from him.

'I've been thinking,' she said, but he was watching her backside in the tight cut-off jeans.

'What?'

'Are you listening to me?' Karen was still smiling, but now she had her hands on her hips.

'Yes, of course I am,' he said, starting to unbuckle his belt.

'Wait. I want to talk to you first.'

Christ, she was starting to sound like his wife now. She walked in front of the car, her legs cutting the beams for a second until she reached the mausoleum. She stood with her back against the white stone, one leg tucked up, her foot flat against the wall, like some old film star from the forties.

He followed her round, trying to fight down the anger.

'What is it, Karen?'

'Oh, don't be like that,' she said, pulling him by the front of his jacket so they were standing close again.

'I love you, and I want you to take me away. I hate my mum and dad. Always asking me to do stuff around the house. I want to be with you where all I'll have to do is make love to you all day, every day.'

His anger ebbed and flowed. This girl knew nothing about real life.

He grabbed her arms and gently pushed her away. 'Karen, this has been fun, but I can't leave my wife. You and I both know that it wouldn't be right.'

'What?' Her eyes went wide. Her face was in shadow, but he could clearly see her eyes. 'You can't mean that!'

Oh shit, her voice was getting higher. There wasn't much chance of anybody hearing her up here, but somebody driving past with a window open and no radio going might.

'It was never meant to be. This was all just a bit of fun. You enjoyed it too, didn't you?'

'Oh, fuck off. I want us to be together, and together we're going to be. You just have to be strong. I know that you can do it. Just tell her. Or do you want me to do it?'

'What? No, of course I don't want you to tell her.' He had to think on his feet now. 'If you really want me to do this, then we have to plan it.'

'You're just saying that.' She was walking backwards now, behind the mausoleum, where the shadows were darker, where the lights from his car didn't reach.

'Come on, Karen, just be sensible about this...' he started to say, but then she screamed.

'What are you doing?' he asked her.

Karen screamed again. 'Please don't leave me!' she shouted at the top of her voice, and he wanted to hold her, he really did, but what he did instead was grab her by the hair and slam her head into the back wall of the mausoleum. Once, twice, three times. Maybe four or five, he couldn't be sure.

She stopped screaming. And slid down the wall, the back of her skull crushed and leaving a mess as she made her way to a sitting position in the grass.

Her eyes were open and he looked into them, calling her name out over and over, fighting down bile and panic.

Then he turned and started to run back to his car, but then forced himself to walk slowly or else he would run as fast as he could and drive as fast as he could, but he couldn't let that happen.

He knew where he had to go. What he had to do. Whom he had to speak to.

His hands were shaking as he tried taking coins out of his pocket. The phone box was in a part of town that had a few businesses, but they were closed for the night. He'd parked round the corner and had walked with his head down, hands in his pockets, as if he was drunk.

He looked at his watch and knew he still had plenty of time. Poker night with some fictitious friends would still go on for hours. The fact he never won didn't seem to bother his wife, as long as he was out of her hair for a little while. She knew how important it was for him to unwind.

He put in the coins, dialled the number and waited for an answer at the other end. His friend had said to call anytime. He was used to getting calls at all hours of the day.

'Hello?' the voice at the other end said.

'It's me.'

'Hello. How are you doing?'

'Fine but not very dandy. I have a problem.'

'Then you've called the right number. I am a person who can help you with that problem. Tomorrow at nine?'

'No, fuck. I need help now. I'm in a bit of a jam,' the man said.

'A jam, you say? How big of a jam?' The friend sounded light and jolly, and the man hoped he hadn't been drinking.

'Can you help me or not? This is big. As big as it gets.'

Silence from his friend. *'I can help with that. Where are you?'*

He told him.

'Hang fire. I'll be there in less than ten. Are you parked nearby?'

'Yes.' He told him where.

'We'll go in your car. Then when we're done, you will drop me off near my car and then we'll go our separate ways.'

'Okay. Anything you want.' He hung up and stood in the call box, as if still talking on the phone. He kept looking outside to see if anybody was coming along to use the phone, but nobody did.

Cars went by, but not the one he was expecting. He knew what his friend drove, and then suddenly it was turning into the street. He walked along to his own car and got in, then the passenger door opened and his friend jumped in.

'Tell me what this jam is then,' his friend asked.

'I'll show you.' He didn't want to explain and then have his friend jump out, knowing what he had just done. This way, if they both went there, then his friend would be an accomplice.

They drove in silence, the headlight beams cutting through the dark in the country lane. Another five minutes and they were going into the cemetery. He was surprised to see his friend looked comfortable being in here. He drove through the arch and headed round to the mausoleum, this time turning the car sideways so the lights shone on the little death house.

'When did you kill her?' his friend asked.

'What?' he said, thinking his friend was going to turn against him. It wasn't too late to just put his foot down and go round in the opposite direction and hightail it out of there so his friend would never see the corpse.

'You call me and we dodge about like government spies and you bring me here in the dark. It's not to invite me to have two's up. So I'll ask you again: when did you kill her?'

'Shortly before I called you.'

'Explain.'

So he did. Right down to the details of where Karen's head was hitting off the stone wall.

'I can help you, but we have to have an understanding.'

'Anything.'

His friend looked at him in the darkness of the car. 'I might want to call in that favour one day. Be prepared. Remember how I came running to help you.'

'I will. Anything you need, just ask.'

'Okay, let's make this right.' His friend stepped out of the car and gently closed the car door without closing it fully.

The man got out, walked over to the mausoleum and went round the back. Karen was still there, still staring at nothing.

'I've heard of rough sex, but you've taken it too far,' the friend said.

The man didn't see the funny side. What if he made up a story instead and said he came here and found his friend had killed the girl, and the friend had tried to kill him, but he had killed the friend instead?

The thought was going through his mind when he was brought back to the present.

'I said, give me a hand to lay her flat. I have an idea.'

'You do?' The man felt a sigh of relief. This was going to be alright after all. Would they bury Karen and wait until she was reported missing? Take her away somewhere and dump her body in the river?

He grabbed an arm while his friend grabbed the other, and they dragged her round to the side of the mausoleum and laid her flat in the grass.

What was the big plan now? He peeked his head round the corner of the stone house and turned back to see his friend with a knife out.

'What are you doing?' he asked, not being able to see what was happening. Then his friend stood up, smiling.

'There you go. Problem solved. They'll think some head case is on the loose.' He stood back to look at his handiwork.

The man looked down at Karen's chest and his breath caught in his throat for a moment. He tried breathing but couldn't. His heart raced and he could feel the heat rising in his face. His whole body felt on fire now.

I am Nightmare was carved into Karen's chest. There wasn't as much blood as some people might think there would be. He knew that because her heart had stopped pumping the blood wouldn't flow. They would know this had been done postmortem.

'What's that?' he said, looking down.

'That's your ticket to freedom. Drive me back down to my car.'

The man hesitated and the friend gently grabbed him by the arm. 'Come on. They'll find her eventually. A dog walker or something. If they don't, we'll make an anonymous tip.'

They walked back to the car and got in. The man had one last look at Karen and then she was in darkness once more as the headlights pointed back the way they had come, until they got to the archway and then he drove just on the sidelights.

He only started breathing when he got to the road, and they drove in silence back to the friend's car. The friend got out and looked back in.

'Don't call me for a few days.'

The man nodded.

And Jeremy Wilson watched as the red taillights disappeared, then he went into the phone box and called treble nine. Took a hanky out and put it over the mouthpiece.

'Hello? Police. I heard a scream over by the old graveyard...'

TWENTY-THREE

Calvin Stewart's eyebrows knitted together as he walked into the dining room and was dismayed to see Dunbar and Evans already seated at a table, a cup of coffee in front of each man. There were no other guests in yet.

'I hope you haven't eaten all the fucking tattie scones,' he said, going over to the flask and pouring himself a coffee.

'He said all the breakfast stuff has been eaten. We had the last of it,' Dunbar said.

'Get tae fuck,' Stewart said, sitting down beside them. 'I know you're pulling my chain. You wouldn't still be sitting here if you'd eaten all the scran.' He looked at Evans. 'What's up with your pus? You look like you're trying to pass a hedgehog.'

'I didn't get much sleep, sir.'

'Well, you either got lucky, which I very much doubt, or else Comrade Dunbar here snores like a bull-dozer starting up.'

Evans said nothing but held on to his coffee cup.

'I, on the other hand, slept like a log, you'll be pleased to know.'

'Why would we be pleased about that, Calvin?' Dunbar asked.

'Because it means I'm in a good mood. And if I'm in a good mood, then nobody gets their fucking arse kicked.' Stewart looked round to the door. 'Where's that fuckin' heid-the-baw with the scran? I told him last night I want some of everything.'

'Good morning, gentlemen,' Shipley's wife said, wheeling in a trolley with plates on it. 'Are your friends coming down?'

'They should be here shortly. They're running a bit late, so we'll just get wired in while we're waiting.'

'Great. If you want anything else, just ring the wee bell on the table.'

'Thanks, hen,' Stewart said, although the woman was older than him by a good ten years.

She put the plates on the table and lifted the big silver platter on. It was covered by a lid, as if it held a turkey under it. Stewart lifted the lid off and handed it to Evans.

'What do you want me to do with that?'

'Shove it up your fucking jacksie for all I care. Sit on it, play drums on it, whatever keeps your pecker up, but just get it out of my way.'

Evans reached round and put it on the table behind them. Then he picked up a fork and was about to spear some bacon.

'Here, here, what are you, a fucking animal?'

'I just want a bit of bacon.'

Stewart started waving his own fork about dangerously. 'Two senior detectives here, son. Get a grip. The pecking order does not go from low to high. DCI Dunbar and I will pick at it and we'll leave something for you. It's the way the hierarchy works.'

Evans snatched a piece of bacon with his fingers and Stewart brought the fork down and missed but hit a slice of black pudding. 'Wee bastard. Dae that again and you'll be wearing the fuckin' thing,' Stewart said, just as Harvey Shipley came into the room. Once again, he looked at Dunbar, silently questioning if Stewart really was polis. And once again, Dunbar only nodded, as if he too had trouble believing it. Shipley nodded back. Brothers in arms.

'Good morning, Superintendent Stewart,' Shipley said with a big smile on his face. 'Can I get you some toast?'

'Smashing, Harv. Wee bit o' marmalade too, if you like.'

'Yes, sir, anything you want.' Shipley rubbed his hands together and beamed a smile, as if he had a meth lab in the basement and was desperate for Stewart not to go poking around down there. He retreated and Dunbar nodded again. He felt they were now part of their own two-man secret society.

'Do you think old Harvey is all there? Is it just me or do you think the cunt talks a bit slow?' Stewart said.

'I think he talks that way because he thinks *you're* slow. Sir,' Evans said.

'You're doing my fucking melon in and it's not even gone eight yet. Try and not make me stab you in the eye with a fork before I've had my first tattie scone.'

'Just an observation, sir.'

Harry, Derek and Jill came into the dining room. Harry had every intention of telling Stewart about the conversation they'd had the night before, about the hidden fingers that were presumably from the three murder victims from thirty years ago.

'I think old Chuckles is away to get more scran. Better claim some grub before Hungry Horace there gets his mitts all over it.' Stewart looked at Evans. 'I hope you washed your hands after playing pocket golf again.'

'No golf this morning, sir.'

Jill walked over to Stewart. 'Calvin, I think we

should sit at a different table. We need to discuss things.'

'Yes, ma'am,' he said, lifting his plate and his coffee mug, and he walked over to Jill's table. They sat down just as Mrs Shipley wheeled in more food under another platter lid. Harry wondered how many they had. Stewart waved the old woman over so Jill could fill her plate, but she didn't want anything. He, on the other hand, took the platter and helped himself to more tattie scones.

Jill went into detail about what had occurred the night before, bringing him up to speed.

'Not sure I agree with Harry chucking out what could have been a key piece of evidence, but it's done now, and he didn't have to tell us, I suppose,' Stewart said, in a rare moment of solidarity. 'So you think the old retired cop was going under the name Eric Straw?' he said.

'We think so.'

Harry's phone rang and he excused himself. Then he came back into the dining room after a couple of minutes.

'Sorry to interrupt, ma'am, but that was the station. The old woman who owns the B&B where Hannah Keddie was living called them and said she found a backpack stuffed in a cupboard in her private quarters. When she opened it, she saw a folder inside. Nearly made her vomit, she said. Filthy pictures of dead people and all sorts of newspaper clippings. I think it might have belonged to Archie Baker.'

'Go over and get it, Harry. Bring it back here. I'm going home to get a change of clothes and a shower, then I'll come back and we can go through that backpack.'

Harry turned from the table and was about to leave the dining room when Derek stood up. 'I'd like to go with you,' he said.

'Come on then.'

Harry told the others to save him some tattie scones.

'Aye, right,' Stewart said.

'Sir, I can't be sure, but I think I saw Harvey licking them before he brought them through.'

'Aw come, McNeil, play the fucking game. Anyway, I've had worse.' He looked at Jill. 'Apologies for the language, ma'am, but my therapist assures me it's a mental illness.'

'That's the least of our worries.'

'You should see where he wiped the bacon,' Harry said as a parting shot.

'Get out, McNeil.'

It felt good to be in the sunshine. Too many cold days in Edinburgh had made Harry sceptical about the impending summer, but now here it was and the sun felt good on his bones.

'You want me to drive?' Derek said.

'I can manage, thank you very much. I didn't have a skinful last night. Just a few sociable beers.'

'Aye, me too.'

They got in the car. 'Tell me you aren't going to confess to anything,' Harry said, starting the car up and slowly pulling out of the small car park.

'No, of course not. Jill and I are just friends.'

'Try and keep it that way. We have enough on our plate without you adding adultery to the mix.'

'Briony and I aren't married, so technically it wouldn't be adultery.'

'Try explaining that to her when she has a carving knife in her hand.'

'I think the boys just retreated back into the fort.'

'Make sure they stay there.'

Harry drove while his brother got Google Maps out and directed them to the B&B. Derek waited in the car while Harry went inside.

Isla Campbell was waiting inside. Her husband ushered Harry through to the private quarters, where a dog came running up to him, wanting to be petted.

Harry obliged as Isla got the backpack.

'I've never seen such filth in my life,' she said, and her husband looked nonchalant, as if he had indeed seen such filth before, probably between the pages of a men's magazine, but he nodded in agreement, lest she start searching for his secret stash.

'That girl seemed nice, but what line of work is this? In my day, you learned to type and sat behind a desk from nine to five. Not like today, messing about on the internet, eking out a living.'

'They didn't have the internet back in your day,' her husband remarked.

'Pedantic. Anyway, I don't know why it was stuffed in a cupboard in my living room. The guests are not permitted back here unless invited. I did invite Hannah through here, so she knew there was a cupboard there. Poor girl.' Isla started to cry and Harry put a hand on her arm.

'Thank you for this. It might help catch her killer.'

'She's been scared out of her wits since she found it this morning. She thinks the killer will come after her now,' the husband said.

'I wouldn't worry about that,' Harry said. 'If you see anything suspicious, call treble nine.'

'And what? They'll find our bodies? Don't worry, I used to be in the army and I always carry a knife.'

Harry was about to give him a lecture on the perils of taking on a mugger, but he thought it would fall on deaf ears, so he just nodded.

'Be careful,' was all he said.

He and Derek drove back to Muir of Ord and waited in the dining room for Jill to come back. The other guests had had a quick breakfast and left. Harry wondered if the French visitor would have survived breakfast if he'd stayed, but the other two guests didn't seem to notice Stewart's sudden outbursts or had been too hungry to be bothered.

'Now you've got me wondering if that old fuck gobbed in the coffee,' Stewart complained, but Harry noticed he had poured himself another anyway.

Jill came back, changed and showered and with renewed vigour.

'Have you looked at the file yet?' she asked.

'No, not yet. We were waiting for you.'

They pulled two tables together and crammed in. Harry had pulled on a pair of nitrile gloves and he opened the zipper on the backpack and gingerly took out the buff folder as if it would explode.

It was the kind with a flap and a piece of elastic wound round a button to keep the flap closed. Harry thought they should get something similar for Stewart's mouth. He passed it to Jill.

She opened it and looked inside, just as Isla Campbell had done. There were newspaper clippings and photos from crime scenes.

'Karen McPherson,' Jill said, looking at the others. 'The first victim.'

She put the crime scene photos down and looked at the words that had been carved into her chest: *I am Nightmare.*

'What about the other two victims?' Harry asked.

'They were found five days later in the same spot. It was the night of the candlelight vigil...'

TWENTY-FOUR

Back then

There were a lot of hands to shake. Being the school psychologist, Jeremy Wilson did the rounds in the park as if this was some kind of macabre social event.

The candlelight vigil had been his idea, suggested to the headteacher, some old ponce who thought he was an astronaut of the teaching world. He went ahead and suggested to the school board they have a candlelight vigil for Karen. It had been unanimously agreed upon, and they bypassed Wilson. He'd smiled a sympathetic smile and agreed to help.

The news had spread and all the kids who attended Dingwall High School attended, even though not everybody knew Karen. She had left school just a couple of weeks previously, ready to take on the world, the headteacher said through his bullhorn. Gaggles of girls huddled together, holding up their candles with drip protectors wrapped round the bottom.

They played music through some speakers in celebration of Karen's life, and not one time did anybody mention that she had been sleeping with a married man and wanted to run away with him. It wasn't the sort of thing anybody would bring up, even if they knew.

Wilson scanned the crowds, hiding in plain sight. Nobody questioned why he was standing on his own, and kids regularly came up to him. Plenty of faces were familiar to him, parents whom he had dealt with in the past. They would later on swear that he had been here and left with one family in particular whose daughter was having nightmares.

He spoke to them, and casually mentioned that there were a lot of unfamiliar faces there too, making it seem as if he was glad of the support.

They would later tell police that there were a lot of strangers there and any one of them could have been the killer.

It couldn't be Wilson. Although they would question him, the family backed his story up: he had left with them and got into his car.

But other people would swear blind they saw a

stranger follow a group of girls. More than one family saw this, and nobody came forward to claim their innocence. To explain to the police that they had just parked their car in a different street and were walking back to it. Maybe they really were a paedophile, or were scared of being labelled as one.

The police were on the hunt for the Nightmare Man, somebody who only existed in fevered minds at night. But for that short period of time, he was very real, and the monster who had been lurking amongst them had come to the surface.

The police sketch artist had been kept busy. Patrols were stepped up, looking for the phantom killer. He was wearing black. He was wearing red. He was tall. He was short. He had dark hair. He had fair hair. They could have told the press he looked like Shrek and nobody would have found him.

Jeremy Wilson added fuel to the fire, saying that he had seen a few strangers, men standing on their own, but he knew a lot of pupils had come to the vigil.

'Could you not have mentioned this to a police officer at the time?' one detective asked.

'Could one of your men who was posted right there not have spotted this?' was Wilson's reply, and that shut them up. Nobody wanted a lawsuit or pointed fingers. So they concentrated on hunting down a monster who didn't exist, and let the one who did exist walk amongst them.

That night had gone well for Wilson. He had got back in his car and had singled out a couple of girls who were walking away on their own. The crowd was thinning out now, and he saw the two girls split off. He knew them and they knew him. That was the key.

Sophie Allander and Josie Brown. Both of them had left high school along with Karen.

Wilson stopped his car as he saw the two girls cutting off the main road and taking a shortcut.

'Girls!' he said after rolling the window down. They turned and walked back to him.

'Hello, Mr Wilson,' they said.

'It's a bit dangerous to be walking here alone, don't you think?'

'There's two of us,' Sophie said. The bigger one. The ballsier one.

'Where are you off to?'

The girls looked at each other as they bent over to look into his car. 'The graveyard. We wanted to say goodbye to Karen privately. Light a candle up where she was murdered.'

Wilson felt a jolt of electricity shoot through him. Would it work? The same place? Not what he had planned, but it might work. He looked in the mirror and saw there was nobody else around. They were on the country road. No traffic.

'You want me to come with you? To make sure you're okay? I mean, I can stay back if you like, if you just want to light a candle.'

They thought about it for a second. 'Okay then,' Sophie said, making the decision for both of them.

They jumped in the back and he took off after another look around.

'She was a nice girl,' Wilson said. 'I couldn't believe it. Not around here. But it's a bad world we live in and it shows you it can happen on our own doorstep. I hope your parents keep your front doors locked.'

He looked in the rear-view mirror at them. They were huddled together.

'They do now,' Josie said.

They made their way into the graveyard and he drove them round to the mausoleum. Crime-scene tape was left over, tied to a tree. A pair of nitrile gloves was on one side in the grass. Wilson's headlights picked out the mausoleum, where Karen had drawn her last breath, and he stopped in front of it.

'This place is creepy,' Josie said.

'Don't be such a baby,' Sophie said, opening the passenger door, and they stepped out into the chill wind.

'You got the matches?' Sophie asked.

'No, I thought you had them?'

'How did you light the candles in the park?' Wilson asked, stepping out onto the grass. He had turned the headlights off but kept the sidelights on. And the engine. Last thing he wanted to do was run the battery down.

'Somebody gave us a light,' Sophie said, throwing her friend a look.

'Just as well I did drive you up here,' Wilson said with a smile, bringing a lighter out. 'Let's get out of the wind and light them round here.'

He led them to the back, where Karen had died. Some of the mess from her head was still on the mausoleum wall. Josie made a face and stepped back round, standing at the side wall.

'Here, let me light this for you,' Wilson said to Sophie and he brought the lighter up and lit the candle.

Sophie thanked him and turned away, shielding the small flame, and started talking as if her friend would hear her.

'I'll go and see if Josie is okay,' he said, and he stepped out of the shadows and round to where the other girl had gone. The sidelights gave a little bit of illumination, but he couldn't see Josie at first.

She was standing smoking a cigarette.

'You okay?' Wilson said.

She jumped, startled for a moment. 'Yes, I'm okay.'

'Good.' He didn't need to explain where he was going, so he just slipped away.

Sophie was still standing with the candle, talking to her dead friend, when Wilson walked quietly up behind her and rammed her head into the back wall of the mausoleum. Unlike Karen, Sophie didn't go down first time.

She dropped the candle and a look of anger swept over her face. Wilson knew that if Sophie's hands got near his face, she could scratch him and that wouldn't be good.

He hit her head against the wall much harder, and then again. That stunned her, but she was still standing. He brought out his little knife, opened it and rammed it into Sophie's neck.

That did the trick. Sophie slid down, just like Karen had.

'Oh my God,' Josie said, stepping round the corner. 'It was you. Oh Jesus, no, please.' She looked at Wilson with the knife still in his hand.

'Josie, I can explain,' he said, but she turned and ran. He wasn't sure if she couldn't scream or was just trying to save her breath or what, but off she went, running back the way they had come.

Josie was wearing dark clothing and it was hard to see her. Fuck, she had dropped out of sight. Brilliant.

Now he was well and truly fucked. He should have kept them close together.

Then he heard a squeal from further along the track and then...two people stepped out from behind a mausoleum.

He thought for a second that it was Sophie as well. That he hadn't killed her, that she had somehow faked it and now she and Josie were about to take him on.

Then he saw it was somebody else holding Josie by the hair. Another girl.

'Kill her,' this stranger said.

Wilson was momentarily taken aback. 'What?'

'Kill her. I saw what you did to Sophie. I was watching. I know you killed Karen. I saw you with that copper the other night. Was he helping you to cover it up?'

Wilson didn't answer but felt his feet carrying him on towards this young woman, who was smiling at him, and now he saw she was holding a knife to Josie's throat. The other girl was begging for her life.

'I used to go to school with them, but I was shy. Nobody took an interest in me. Especially those three bitches. So them being murdered is a good way for them to go.'

Wilson had planned on killing the two girls to make it look like a maniac was on the loose. It was no big deal for him. After all, he'd killed before.

'Are you going to kill her as well?' the young woman said. 'No? Then let me help you.' She drew the knife across Josie's throat and a huge gush of blood shot into the air. Josie gasped for breath and clutched at her neck before falling onto her knees. Then onto her face as the blood flowed out of her.

Wilson stood looking at her before taking a few steps towards the woman.

'How do you know I won't just kill you as well?' he asked her, watching as the life ebbed out of Josie and she became still.

'How do you know I won't kill you?' she asked him.

Wilson didn't have the answer. Maybe he should just kill her and clean up all the loose ends, of which she had become the latest.

'You're very trusting,' he said, the wind whipping the trees now.

'You are too.'

'Fair point. But let's get this young lady round beside her friend.'

Wilson was reaching down to grab the young girl by the shoulders when the other young woman grabbed him, putting an arm around his neck. Then she brought the knife round and brought it across his throat.

'That was the blunt side, obviously,' she said to him, laughing. 'I think we can trust each other. And even if you don't trust me yet, you have to understand that I left insurance behind. A notebook detailing all my thoughts and suspicions. If I die, they'll go through my things and then they'll find the notebook. Let me say, it's just until we get to know each other better.'

He got over his initial anger and smiled. He'd have to get a notebook of his own.

'Help me lift her,' he said, and they carried the body back round to where Sophie was.

And the Nightmare Man became legend.

TWENTY-FIVE

Alex had been happy that Harry had called her, and now she felt bored again. The baby was a lot harder work than she had anticipated, but it was like running a relay race: a frantic burst of energy and then quiet. She loved her daughter more than anything in the world, but she was still debating about returning to work or not. It wasn't a decision that could be made lightly. Harry would love nothing more than for her to stay at home, but being a detective was *part* of her. She didn't think Harry understood.

She went through to the kitchen, where she took some more painkillers. She used to get migraines a long time ago, but they had faded. Now with all this added stress of having to rethink her career choices, they were back with a vengeance.

'Just relax, Alex,' she said out loud to herself.

Grace was getting tired again. One last look out of the window over to the bowling green where Mummy and Daddy used to go for a good drink at the weekend, and then off to bed.

'I love you, little Gracie.'

She laughed. Harry hated Alex calling the baby that. It was Grace or nothing, he had said.

She got a text from Harry.

Just wanted to say I love you. Xxx

Love you too, honey. Don't ever forget that. xxx

She was just getting baby Grace down for a nap when the doorbell rang. 'Oh, who the hell is this?' she said, thinking that her daughter was going to wake up, but the baby was sound asleep. Alex left her in the cot while she went to get rid of the unwanted visitor.

She opened the door and was about to explain when she stopped in her tracks.

She was about to protest, to say something, but she thought of the baby for a second, and then the figure was inside.

TWENTY-SIX

'Jeremy Wilson killed those girls,' Jill said, putting down a notebook. 'According to Archie Baker. That was his theory.'

'He didn't have any real proof, though,' Harry said. 'However, why start the killing again? Somebody was getting close to an answer, and that was Hannah Keddie. I think she got close enough to spook the killer.'

'I don't think it's Jeremy Wilson,' Dunbar said. 'There's no way he survived that fire and rubble coming down on top of him.'

'Look at those notes,' Stewart said, drinking more coffee. 'Baker said they found two sets of prints at the scene the second time round. Was he working with somebody? Was he working with somebody when Karen McPherson was killed and they just didn't find

the different shoe prints? It had been raining the day of
the second killings, it says in the report.'

'One shoe print was smaller,' Evans said.

'Where does your dad fit into all of this, Harry?
And Willie Dowd? And my dad?' Jill said.

'Wilson told me he was keeping them all under
control. If Wilson got caught, he would try and take
them all down for murder. Obviously, Wilson had
hidden the finger somewhere close to Willie Dowd,
and then he put it in his new car, and maybe forgot to
take it back out. Or, more likely, didn't know Willie
was going to sell it. That's why he took it from the
garage where I had it stored and was running about in
it. He left the finger there, maybe hoping it would still
drop my dad in it.'

'Somebody still wants the secret kept,' Dunbar
said.

'I think I know who,' Harry said.

TWENTY-SEVEN

Auntie Ella had already pissed herself once, so she told herself that if she did it again, then it wouldn't matter.

'If he doesn't come, then you're going to have to call him,' her attacker said.

'He said he'll be round after breakfast.'

'Tick-tock, the clock is slowly moving forward, one second at a time.' The attacker held the knife to Ella's throat. Just like she'd held the knife to Josie Brown's throat in the cemetery all those years ago.

Ella prayed that her death would be swift.

'You'd better watch that boy of yours. You never know what deviants are going about. You wouldn't want any harm to come to him, would you?'

'Shut up, old woman. He's outside so he doesn't see what's going to happen to you and Harry McNeil.'

Ella laughed. 'All it takes is one second for somebody to snatch him. Then he'll be gone. Out of your life forever.'

'She's right, Lisa,' Harry said, coming into the living room. Lisa Wilson, Jeremy's wife and Willie Dowd's daughter, turned to face him.

'Nobody's going to take him from me. Not if they know better,' she said, but then Ella's back door in the kitchen opened and Robbie Evans walked in, holding Farquhar Wilson's hand. The little boy who had not so long ago been given the name Punching Man because of the habit he had of punching men in the privates.

'Don't you touch him!' Lisa said, putting the knife back to Ella's throat. 'You weren't man enough to come all by yourself,' she said.

'Wasn't Jeremy man enough to kill those women by himself all those years ago?' said Harry.

'He was more of a man than you'll ever be.'

'I think you became the more dominant partner, though, don't you? It's easy to see you were the driving force behind the Tattoo Artist. Great idea, to carry on cutting off fingers. But why don't you and I have this little chat by ourselves? Just you and me? Let Ella go and take me instead.'

Lisa licked her lips. 'No. Let Farquhar go, or I kill the old woman and then I'll fucking kill you both.'

Harry looked at Evans and gave a slight nod. Lisa

was too strong-willed to buckle. This was their only chance.

Farquhar came running over to his mummy and put his arms around her. Evans backed away and left through the back door, closing it quietly behind him.

'I told Jeremy he should have killed you,' Lisa said.

'Ten out of ten for trying. He did his best in your dad's woodworking basement. But I have to say, that was a superb piece of acting when you first came to me and said you thought your dad was a serial killer. Taking me to see the photos from the crime scenes. Except I had my doubts that they were from crime scenes. Not in the traditional sense. Did Willie really take those photos or was it Jeremy?'

'It was my dad. That part was real. But he remained friends with Archie Baker. They kept notes. Then when my dad passed, I get an email from Baker out of the blue. Wanting to know if I'd be interested in talking about the original killings. Saying that he had new information. Turns out, he didn't have anything. It was a bluff, meant to get me up there. It still worked, because I couldn't let him go about digging up dirt on that case.'

'Why didn't you just get rid of the photos that you found in your dad's basement workshop?'

'I didn't find them, I put them there. Daft old sod had them in a drawer. With his dementia, I couldn't risk him talking. He spoke of the murders one day when he was in the home, and he mentioned the photos. I couldn't take the risk. I had to divert attention away from me, so what better way to start out than by hitting the problem head on? I had to make you think Willie was the killer. That was Jeremy's idea. He was the psychologist after all.'

'When I confronted Jeremy in the workshop, he said he married you to keep Willie quiet, and that Colin Harris had taken off Jill Craig's sister's finger and feet. That Jeremy himself was in control of everything. Getting Robert Briggs to write books with him, keeping him in line.'

'Jeremy did like to tell a tale. I fell in love with Jeremy the minute I saw him kill that girl, Sophie, in the graveyard. I had had urges for a long time, and when I saw Jeremy killing, my insides exploded. I knew I had to be with him for the rest of my life. Turned out, it was for the rest of *his* life. Thanks to you. So when I heard from Baker, I wrote back, and he told me he had created an alter ego called Eric Straw. He wasn't sure Hannah Keddie was on board, so I came up here and spray-painted those graves with *I am Nightmare*. That got her arse up here quick enough.'

Harry looked at the little boy. 'Look what you're doing to your son. He's going to be traumatised.'

'No, he's not. He'll be fine.' She looked at him for a

second and smiled, then back at Harry, the knife never moving very far from Ella's throat. 'When I told you that Jeremy didn't want kids, and that I deceived him and fell pregnant, that was the truth. Jeremy didn't want to produce offspring who could turn out to be a killer like us.'

The little boy laughed. 'Uncle Jimmy!'

Lisa was caught off guard for a second and Harry launched himself at his aunt, knocking her off the chair, rolling with her just as Lisa brought the knife round. A second earlier and it would have sliced Ella's throat, but she was falling to the floor.

Dunbar grabbed Lisa's arm as she took a swing at him, and the front door crashed open with Stewart barging in. Evans was past him, helping with the struggling Lisa.

'Right, ya bastard, you're under arrest,' Stewart shouted, just in case anybody was in any doubt about the situation.

Punching Man ran across and punched Stewart in the balls.

'Fuck me,' he said, and Jill Craig grabbed hold of the little boy before he could do more damage and took him outside. Sergeant Bobby McGuire was there with more uniforms and they rushed in to help Evans and Dunbar. Lisa was fighting like she was on drugs.

Harry helped Ella to her feet. 'You little cow,' Ella

said. 'Willie should have skelped your bloody arse when you were a bairn. I remember what a bloody wee toerag you were. It doesn't surprise me you turned out the way you did.'

'Shut up,' Lisa said when she was dragged to her feet, still struggling. Then Lisa looked at Harry. 'You think this is over?' She laughed.

'I would say so.'

'You think Jeremy killed Karen McPherson, the first victim from thirty years ago? Think again. She was shagging a married man. Wanted to run away with him. He didn't want to and he killed her. He said it was accidental, but later admitted he couldn't let her tell his wife.'

'Oh yeah?' Stewart said. 'What's his name?'

She laughed again. 'Harry's wife knows him. His name is Kevin Maxwell. Only she knows him as Dad.'

TWENTY-EIGHT

Harry felt like his whole body was made of ice and he was walking in slow motion as he took his phone outside. Of all his team members, he knew Eve Bell and Ronnie Vallance lived closest.

'Eve...it's...eh, Harry...Harry McNeil...'

Dunbar took his phone from him. 'DS Bell, it's DCI Dunbar here. Alex is in danger. Harry called and can't get hold of her. There's been a credible threat. Are you able to attend Harry's flat?'

'*Fuck me,*' Eve said. '*Yes, of course I can go. I'll call Ronnie Vallance and get control to send a patrol there. I'll get the whole fucking team. Oh Jesus Christ, the bairn. I'll call the whole cavalry. I'll call you back.*'

She hung up.

'Help's on its way, Harry. I'll try Alex again.'

Dunbar called the number and listened to the phone ring at the other end before going to voicemail.

'No answer,' he said, handing Harry his phone back. Harry walked away. Dunbar turned round as Lisa Wilson was brought outside. He walked up to her.

'If something has happened to Alex, you can count on one thing: you'll never see your fucking son again. I'll have him wrapped up in so much red tape, you'll forget what he ever looked like.'

'Fuck you, I know my rights,' she said, and spat in his face.

Dunbar took a hanky out and wiped his face as she struggled with the uniforms.

'You okay?' Robbie Evans said.

'That bastard. I wish I could delay her lawyer and spend some time alone with her. I know people, Robbie. That bastard will be going into general population and I'll make sure the message gets out that she's a fucking kiddie fiddler.'

Stewart came out. 'Fuck me. How can a wee laddie have such a punch? Now, if it was a grown man who did that, he'd be in a fucking wheelchair afterwards. Where's Harry?'

'Over by the car. Ella's in the ambulance and he's saying goodbye to her. We're going down to Edinburgh. Can you wrap things up here with Jill Craig?'

'This is no' my first fitbae game, son. And I'll get

that lassie Liz Aitken to make sure it's escorts all the way. You'll be there in half the time.' Stewart looked at his watch. 'Keep me in the fucking loop. If Alex's old man has harmed her, there won't be one fucking cop in Scotland who isn't looking for the fucker. Right, get going. I'll see you back at home. Tell Harry I'll be thinking of him.'

Dunbar and Evans walked away and got into Harry's pool car.

The first escort was waiting on the Kessock Bridge. That was all Harry remembered of the start of the journey.

Then he got the phone call.

TWENTY-NINE

As hospitals went, the Western General on Crewe Road South was a good one. Their head injury unit was one of the best.

The escort stopped right at the Anne Ferguson Building. Dunbar and Evans had taken turns at driving, while Harry sat in the back talking to Ronnie Vallance on the phone.

When they got into the building, a doctor was waiting for Harry. He took them upstairs. Eve Bell and Vallance were waiting for them.

It was the first time Harry had seen Ronnie Vallance crying.

'Aw fuck,' Dunbar said, his own face starting to crumble. He looked at Evans and saw tears running down his face.

'Grace is fine,' Eve said. 'The nurses have her.'

Harry nodded and mouthed *thank you*, not trusting his voice at this point.

The doctor took Harry into a room, but Harry stopped him. 'Jimmy, can you come in with me? I might miss what's being said.'

Dunbar nodded. They sat down and Harry half listened to the doctor.

'It was a cerebral haemorrhage. It was obviously undetected, as so many of them are. It ruptured, causing massive brain damage. If she were to wake up, she would be in a complete vegetative state for the rest of her life. But she's not going to wake up.'

Harry sat staring. So many questions, but he couldn't even ask one.

'What would cause it to rupture?' Dunbar said.

'Most likely a sudden increase in blood pressure. Like if she got excited or angry.'

'Or scared?' Harry asked.

'Perhaps, but it's most likely if she had been arguing with somebody, for instance. That sort of thing would cause it. But it was a ticking time bomb in her head. It literally could have ruptured at any time.'

'What now, Doc?' Dunbar asked.

'We need Mr McNeil's permission to switch off life support.'

Tears rolled down Harry's cheeks. 'There's no way she could have a miracle recovery?'

'I'm afraid not. We've done all the tests. Your wife is officially brain dead. There's no sign of activity. The machines are keeping her alive just now.'

Dunbar put a hand on Harry's arm. 'I'm right here, pal.'

Harry nodded. 'As her next of kin, I give you permission. But I want to see her first.'

'Of course.'

They left the room. Robbie Evans was sitting in the hallway, knees up, his head in his hands, his shoulders shaking as he quietly sobbed.

A nurse led Harry and Dunbar into a room. 'My daughter. Where is she?' Harry asked.

'She was taken to a paediatric ward. She's fine.' I'll leave you alone now.'

Harry nodded and then gave his full attention to Alex. Hooked up to monitors and whatever else it took to keep somebody breathing while their brain was dead.

'I love you,' he said, reaching out to hold her hand. 'I wish you didn't have to go. Our wee girl is going to grow up knowing who her mum was. I'll make sure of that. God, how am I going to go on without you? You made me such a better person.'

Just then, the door opened. Harry's son, Chance, came in, his face a train wreck.

'Dad, what happened?' he said, throwing himself at his father.

'An aneurysm burst in her brain.'

'Is she going to be alright? They won't tell me anything.'

Harry looked his son in the eyes. 'She's brain dead. They're going to switch off life support.'

'Oh God,' Chance said, looking at his stepmother. 'I can't believe this.' He walked forward and held her hand. He stood like that for what seemed like an eternity. 'I love you, Alex. I will never forget you.'

He was crying when he reached over and kissed her forehead, and a tear fell on her cheek, like she was the one who was crying.

Chance left and the doctor came in.

Dunbar kissed her forehead. 'Sleep tight, beautiful lassie. We're going to miss you.'

He patted Harry on the shoulder and left the room.

'What now?' Harry said to the doctor, his voice thick.

'We turn the machines off. But take whatever time you need, Mr McNeil. There's no rush. Spend some time with your wife. Tell the nurse when you're ready and I'll come back. In your own time.' He quietly left the room.

Harry was alone with Alex now and he sat in a chair next to her bed and held her hand. Her face was so peaceful looking. Her eyes were closed and he couldn't believe that he would never see her smile again. Or hold her or tell her that he loved her. She would never see their little girl grow up. She would never see Grace go to school, or dance at her wedding.

Never help their little girl blow out the candles on her first birthday cake. Watch her take her first steps or walk her to school for the first time.

'I promise you that Grace will never forget who you are, sweetheart,' he said, his voice a dry whisper. 'I keep pinching myself, thinking this is a nightmare. That I'm going to wake up and you'll be here with me. Oh God, Alex, I love you so much. I fell in love with you and wanted to spend the rest of my life with you. I wanted to grow old with you. I can't believe you're leaving without me.'

He held her hand tight, feeling the warmth in it, knowing it was going to be cold soon. He put his head down on top of her covers and he cried until he couldn't cry anymore.

Later, when he was thinking of this time, replaying everything in his mind, he wouldn't know how long he'd been like that.

But he held her hand and sat there. Until it was time.

He slowly raised his head and wiped away the tears from his face. He gently let go of her hand and opened the room door. The nurse was waiting outside. He nodded to her.

A few minutes later, the doctor came in.

'How long will she have after...?' He couldn't finish the sentence.

'Minutes,' the doctor said. 'She's brain dead so she doesn't know how to breathe on her own. She isn't in pain and she won't feel anything. Are you ready?'

Harry nodded and held on to Alex's hand again as the doctor switched off the machine. The doctor stood at the back of the room as a nurse came in.

'I love you, sweetheart,' Harry said to his wife.

And then Alex left this life for a better one.

The doctor pronounced time of death and he and the nurse left the room.

Harry looked at his wife for the last time. 'I promise I'll look after Grace.'

He walked to the door and turned once, and Alex was standing there looking at him, smiling. 'I know you will, Harry.'

THIRTY

Kevin Maxwell had gone home that day after leaving his daughter on the floor of the living room. It would be weeks before Harry could hear any details of how Eve Bell had got the key from a neighbour and let herself in to find Alex lying on the living room floor.

The neighbour had heard shouting and arguing before she heard the front door opening and closing. Vallance turned up to find Eve and a couple of uniforms on their knees.

The ambulance crew took Alex round to the Western General, two minutes' drive away.

Vallance spoke to Harry on the phone. They sent a patrol car to Kevin Maxwell's house in Dalkeith.

They kicked the front door in. Alex's mother had been murdered by her husband. He'd put a plastic bag over her head before slitting his wrists.

Before he killed himself, he'd taken the knife, and from the blood in the bathroom sink, they surmised he'd looked into it while carving the words into his chest:

I am Nightmare.

AFTERWORD

Ah, the beautiful Scottish Highlands. What can I say? I first started going up there in the late '80's and fell in love with the place. When I met my American wife, I took her to Inverness and she fell in love with the Highlands. We stayed in the Mercure (it had a different name back then) and it was a wonderful experience, especially since my mother was born along the road in Fort George. I wanted to take Harry back and it was a pleasure writing about him in a different locale again.

Some people absolutely hated DSup Stewart in the last book, but a lot of people loved him, and since I have the deciding vote, I brought him back. No doubt we'll see him again.

To kill Alex off or not? That was the decision. But I decided to move the story arc along and we'll see how Harry copes with being a widower and single father.

Thank you to my advanced reader team. You're all magic. A big thanks to Liz Aitken and Jim Brown. Thanks to my family in Scotland. And to my wife Debbie.

A huge shout out to the team at Damonza for the covers. And to my editor, Charlie Wilson. Once again, she stepped up to the plate.

And last but not least, to you, the reader. I hope you enjoyed this book, and if I may ask you to leave a review or rating on Amazon or Goodreads, that would be fabulous. Many thanks in advance.

Stay safe my friends.

John Carson
July 2021
New York

Made in the USA
Monee, IL
21 July 2021

74069471R00134